THE BRICK MAN 4

Lock Down Publications and Ca$h
Presents
THE BRICK MAN 4
A Novel by *King Rio*

Lock Down Publications
P.O. Box 944
Stockbridge, Ga 30281
www.lockdownpublications.com

Copyright 2022 by King Rio
The Brick Man 4

First Edition May 2022
Printed in the United States of America

Lock Down Publications
Like our page on Facebook: Lock Down Publications @
www.facebook.com/lockdownpublications.ldp
Book interior design by: **Shawn Walker**

Stay Connected with Us!

Text **LOCKDOWN** to 22828 to stay up-to-date with new releases, sneak peaks, contests and more...

Thank you!

Submission Guideline.

Submit the first three chapters of your completed manuscript to ldpsubmissions@gmail.com, subject line: Your book's title. The manuscript must be in a .doc file and sent as an attachment. Document should be in Times New Roman, double spaced and in size 12 font. Also, provide your synopsis and full contact information. If sending multiple submissions, they must each be in a separate email.

Have a story but no way to send it electronically? You can still submit to LDP/Ca$h Presents. Send in the first three chapters, written or typed, of your completed manuscript to:

LDP: Submissions Dept
P.O. Box 944
Stockbridge, Ga 30281

DO NOT send original manuscript. Must be a duplicate.

Provide your synopsis and a cover letter containing your full contact information.

Thanks for considering LDP and Ca$h Presents.

King Rio

Prologue

"I really want to see that new Will Smith movie," Shawnna said, eyeing the pickle she was holding up in front of her mouth and preparing to take another bite out of it. *"Collateral Beauty."*

"You look like the star of *Collateral Ugly*," Dawn said without looking up from her iPhone.

Shawnna cut a tight glance at her twin sister. It was 7:00 p.m. Christmas Eve in Chicago, and the Wilkins twins were sitting on opposite ends of the red leather sofa in the living room of their three-bedroom apartment, which was on the second floor in a Drake Avenue building owned by their father, Lee "Juice" Wilkins Sr.

They had planned on attending a Christmas party tonight, but their plans were canceled when, just over six hours ago, a gunman in a black pickup truck had pulled up in front of their building, stuck a gun out his window, and opened fire, not only wounding the guy who was obviously his intended target - Jahlil Owens, their friend Tirzah's husband, had been shot five times - but also wounding two others, including their father.

Juice only suffered a graze wound to the shoulder, and Wayno, who was a high-ranking member of the Traveling Vice Lords gang that Juice ran, had taken a bullet to the wrist. All of this had occurred in a matter of seconds, and Shawnna had watched it all go down while standing at her living room window eating a pickle. Not just any pickle, either. She liked pickles impaled by the straight ends of candy canes. If there wasn't any peppermint in her pickle, she didn't want anything to do with it.

She'd been standing at the window eating her second pickle of the day, parting the blinds with her free hand, wishing she was nine months pregnant instead of four so she could give birth and get back to smoking weed and drinking liquor. Her eyes had settled on a group of teenage boys who appeared to be selling drugs at the other end of the block. Then Jah and his fine-ass brother Rell had pulled up, and her dad and Wayno's equally fine-ass had come trotting out of the building carrying two cardboard boxes. She remembered briefly wondering what was inside the boxes just as the pickup truck came to a stop. That's when the gunfire had begun, the pickup truck driver firing at Jah, Juice, and Wayno, and Jah's big brother firing back at the pickup truck as it raced off down the street. It couldn't have lasted more than five seconds.

Now Jah was in critical condition at Northwestern Memorial Hospital. Juice had thrown the cardboard boxes onto the back seat of his Jaguar SUV and left with his girlfriend, Bubbles, and her twelve-year-old daughter, and he'd told Shawnna and Dawn not to leave the house, so they hadn't left the house.

"I'd hit you in the head with this pickle if it didn't taste so good," Shawnna said to her sister. "You've been talking real crazy lately. Don't get mad at me 'cause you ain't been getting no sex."

"Well, I *would* be getting sex… if you hadn't shot my boyfriend's baby-mama. He hasn't talked to me ever since that day."

"She deserved it," Shawnna reasoned, and took another chunk out of her pickle. "Nobody beats up on you. Not unless it's me."

"That's a fucked-up thing to say. How about *nobody* beats up on me? I like that much better."

"I just said that."

"You're underestimating me," Dawn said. She raised her head and regarded Shawnna with a sneaky little smirk. "You may have won all the fights we had in the past, but it's a new day, baby. You're at a disadvantage now. I'll kick your pregnant ass all through this house."

"You wish," Shawnna said, and burst out laughing. She couldn't help it.

Dawn didn't laugh, but she smiled, at least, and leaned back on the sofa. "I'm worried about Myesha. You and her are both four months pregnant, and she's been our friend since preschool, yet she hasn't been over here to kick it with us in months. I find that strange, Shawnna. Really strange. Don't you? I mean, if she's embarrassed because she let some bum-ass nigga put a baby in her, that's a personal problem. She shouldn't be taking it out on us, though. We've been there for her ass every step of the way. I'm starting to really think she's turned on us, like she has some kind of beef with us or something. I'm not feeling it. I'm ready to confront her about it too."

Shawnna shrugged and made a waving-away gesture, and Dawn sailed on.

"I know what you mean. Trust me, I'm not *at all* pressed about what she's got going on over there. We got enough going on with our hair salon. But I just don't feel like she's being a real friend to us anymore. She found out she was pregnant two days after you did, and she hasn't been over here ever since."

"Friends grow apart."

"You're right. They do. But not childhood friends. Not friends who've known each other since preschool. I'm telling you, she has something on her chest. I don't know if it's something we did, something she *thinks* we did...I don't know. But it's something. A blind man can see that much."

Shawnna shrugged again. Her eyes were on the TV. She'd purchased a bootleg copy of *Almost Christmas* from an old man who always brought cheap stuff into the hair salon to sell to the ladies, a sixty-year-old who'd been known as Old Man Rob until he'd decided to change his name to Django for some odd reason. But she wasn't watching the movie. She was thinking about her good friend Myesha.

This wasn't their first-time discussing Myesha's sudden departure from their tight-knit circle of friends. Dawn brought it up at least once or twice a week, and their mother, Shakela (who'd recently divorced and left their father for another woman, but that was a whole other story), mentioned it just about every time they talked to her.

As much as Shawnna pretended like she didn't care about Myesha's absence from her life, deep down she was really hurt by it. Especially since she didn't know *why* Myesha had decided to stop coming around. Shawnna suspected it might be because Myesha was jealous that they now owned a hair salon that happened to be right across the street from the strip club where she worked. A second theory was that Myesha was upset over the fact that she was pregnant by Lenny, a dude from Detroit who was a manager at White Castle and sold weed as a side hustle, while Shawnna was knocked up by Bankroll Reese, the multimillionaire who actually *owned* the strip club where Myesha had danced all the way up until her tenth week of pregnancy.

"Honestly," Shawnna said dishonestly, "I don't give a fuck *what's* going on with Myesha. She can go to Hell with a gasoline-soaked tampon jammed up her pussy, as far as I'm concerned. We're clearing $4,800-a-month off booth rent alone, plus whatever we make from doing hair ourselves, and that's really all that matters. We're eating good over here. Let that hoe stay mad."

"You don't mean that."

"Yes the hell I do."

"No, the hell you don't. We both love her like a sister, and you know it. She's acting that way for a reason. What we need to be doing is getting her on the phone so we can work through this. Real friends don't give up on each other like this. We ride through thick and thin."

"I tried calling that phony hoe. *Several* times." Another bite of the deliciously sweetened pickle. Crunch-crunch-crunch-crunch-crunch. "I'm not about to be kissing her ass."

"Let's both..." Dawn trailed off.

"Let's both what?" Shawnna asked. "Call her?"

"Do something." Dawn sounded absent, not really in the conversation. She was looking at the screen of her iPhone. Then she looked up at Shawnna. Shawnna could almost see a lightbulb appearing over Dawn's head, like in a cartoon. And there was a light in Dawn's eyes. One that suggested she had one of those genius ideas she was known for coming up with. Growing up, she'd always been the one to come up with the best ideas.

"Hand me your phone," she proposed, smiling into Shawnna's eyes.

"Why?"

"So I can text her the exact same message from both phones. I'll type 'Call me right now' in all caps with exclamation marks. Then we'll call her from your phone."

"I don't know if that's a——"

"It is, though," Dawn said. She was warming to her own inspiration, and when people do that, they rarely take no for an answer. "It's a *great* idea. We'll call from your phone because she'd never be scared of me. She'll answer because she'll see from the text messages that we're together and we're both pissed. When she answers, just be yourself. The angry bitch who's bullied me for half my life. She'll fess up. I guarantee it."

"All right," Shawnna said, handing her phone to Dawn. "Go ahead. Text the bitch." She felt something that might have been mean-spirited gladness. She'd been wanting to get the jealous bitch on the phone for several months now, and the possibility of doing it on a day like today, when she was feeling hormonally evil and irritated, brought a sly grin to her pickle-devouring mouth.

While Dawn typed, Shawnna wondered what her baby's father was doing at the moment. He was currently in New York on a business trip. He was looking to open a new strip club in Harlem and a new nightclub in Queens. She'd Facetimed with him a few minutes after the shooting, and he had almost canceled two meetings to fly back to Chicago. She'd eventually talked him out of it. He would be boarding a private jet to Chicago in less than thirty minutes, according to the text he'd sent her an hour ago, which meant he'd be pulling up by 9:00.

"There," Dawn said briskly. "Both texts have been read. Give it thirty seconds or so. Let her really start getting worried, you know what I mean? I bet her brain's doing backflips right now. Whatever she's got against us is about to come out." She handed Shawnna's phone back, and they waited ten or fifteen seconds, sitting on their large leather sofa in their black flannel pajamas with the words Good Morning Gorgeous written all over them in gold lettering.

Then Shawnna's phone rang.

It was Myesha calling.

"Put on your tough voice, put on your tough voice!" Dawn said, bouncing around excitedly.

"Shhh. Shut the fuck up so I can answer it," Shawnna snapped.

"Okay, okay," Dawn whispered. She made a charming little pantomime gesture of shutting her mouth, turning the key in the middle of her lips, and then throwing the key back over her shoulder.

Shawnna answered the call and immediately heard crying on the other end, but she didn't let that throw her off. "You know you got me *fucked* up, right? You can save that crybaby bullshit for somebody who cares, 'cause bitch, I stopped caring when you stopped calling, and now that I've found out about all this bullshit, I've *really* stopped caring."

"*How was I supposed to tell you?*" Myesha screamed through the phone. "How could I tell my best friend in the whole fucking world that I'm pregnant by the same man she's pregnant by? How could I tell *you* that? You should've *killed* me."

Shawnna's mouth was wide open, as it had been since she'd heard the second question, and her eyes were on Dawn.

Myesha went on, explaining how she and Reese's scandalous affair had begun one late night at his Burr Ridge mansion, unaware that Shawnna was no longer listening to her. Shawnna was now employing all her mind, all her considerable powers of thought, to make herself believe that she wasn't going to have to exterminate her childhood friend. *Exterminate* was a word her subconscious had been more than eager to cast up, because in her mind, Myesha had just turned into a roach, and the inclination to squash that bug-bitch under her shoe was suddenly overwhelming.

King Rio

Chapter 1

Juice had never settled on the right word for the place where Bubbles lived. It was too big to be called a house, too small to be called an estate, and the name on the post at the foot of the driveway, Masterdeen, made him clench his teeth every time he saw it. It sounded too much like the name of a mean old slave owner from the 1800s, the kind who might crack you with the whip in the morning and crack your woman with the dick in the night. He usually wound up just calling it "your place," as in "let's go to your place and watch the game" or, more commonly, "let's go to your place and fuck."

It was pretty much the same deal with Bubbles herself, he thought, watching her reflection in the dresser mirror as she sat on his lower back in her bra and thong panties, rubbing his upper back, where the tension was. You didn't want to call your girlfriend by her stripper name, but when reverting to her real name meant Lakita, and your ex-wife's name was Shakela, it left you with no real ground to stand on.

He wasn't big on expressing feelings. He knew she wanted to hear him say he loved her, especially on Christmas Eve - surely a better present than the diamond tennis bracelet he'd purchased her, although the bracelet had set him back a teeth-clenching amount - but he couldn't do it. He couldn't bring himself to say, "I love you, Bubbles." The best he could manage was "I fuck with you the long way, baby." And not even he was certain what that meant.

He did love her, though. He'd said it once or twice before, but now he was reluctant to say it again. For one thing, he thought she was still a little hung up on a guy she used to date, a guy who happened to be one of the wealthiest men in America. They'd returned home from a trip to California early this morning, and during the trip, her wealthy ex - Grammy

Award-winning rap artist Blake "Bulletface" King - had become his new cocaine plug. For another, Juice had recently gone through a messy divorce, and he wasn't in a hurry to take that walk again anytime soon.

"You don't think that shooting was connected to that boy Jah killed on 15th Street, do you?" she asked. "I mean, the man was obviously targeting Jah. He *had* to be targeting Jah to shoot him five times, don't you think?"

"Ain't no telling. Jah done popped up a whole lotta people. It could be revenge for some shit that happened last year. Or it might've just been some gangbangin' shit that didn't really have shit to do with none of us. You never know. All I can say is they better hope Jah don't make it, because if he lives, it is going to get ugly." Juice had an unlit Cuban cigar held between the middle and forefingers of his right hand. He'd taken a shower about thirty minutes ago and all he wore now was an expensive pair of silk Versace boxer shorts. Bubbles had coated him with lotion and now his bald head gleamed like Steve Harvey's. "I got security at both ends of the block now, so we'll be good."

"You sure about that?"

"I wouldn't say it if I wasn't."

"You won't know if somebody's about to start shooting until somebody pulls a gun and starts shooting. It's not like the shooter is gonna tell your boys - your *security* - that he has a gun and is about to use it. I think it might be best if you moved your daughters out of that building. It's not safe, in my opinion."

"Their salon is right around the corner from the house," Juice said, turning over on his back. "And besides, I'll be damned if I let a nigga run me or my family out of my neighborhood. We'll catch up with whoever did the shooting. The streets talk. Somebody'll say something. Wayno saw that

16

same truck riding up and down 16th last night, so we know for sure he had to be looking for Jah if it took him that long to finally get to shooting."

"I bet it's because of Jamal."

"Forget about Jamal."

"How can I forget about Jamal when I watched him get his brains blown out two days ago?"

"You didn't see that. Neither did I. And I don't wanna ever hear you say it again. That's the kinda talk that can get a man a hundred years. We don't do that kinda talk."

She sighed and rested her hands on her knees, gazing down at him with her bottom lip between her teeth. Her thighs were as full and meaty as her butt. She had small breasts that stood out from her chest in perfect perky swells. Her skin was smooth and flawless, the complexion of peanut butter. She had the face of an angel - or at least that's how Juice saw it. If he ever made it to Heaven, he hoped to find it full of beautiful black women like her. That would make all the hell he went through in the land of the living worth it.

"I'm sorry," she said. "You're right. I just feel like I should be able to talk about anything with my man."

"You can, but let's keep the focus on us moving forward. That's what's important ain't it?

She nodded. "So what's the deal with you and Blake? Did he take Hector's place as your connect for the good stuff? Or is that also none of my business?"

"Nah, we can talk about it." He slid his hands up and down her thighs. "He let me get a better deal than the one I had with Hector. I should be able to reach my goal by the end of January."

"And then you're done, right?"

"And then I'm done."

She regarded this with some skepticism, sucking her teeth and squinting. He'd promised to give up the street life once he had ten million dollars saved up, and right now he had a little over two. His trap houses were adding on average of $20,000 to his savings every day. But that number was about to go way up, thanks to his new plug, who had blessed him with the keys to a vacant Highland Park mansion that had 1,000 kilograms of cocaine stuffed inside a hundred cardboard boxes in the garage. Blake wanted $10,000 for every kilo. With kilos currently going for $36,000 all across the city of Chicago, it would be quite easy for Juice to reach his ten-million-dollar goal. In fact, he could very easily *double* his goal. As long as he managed to keep the Feds out of his business, he could be sitting on a good forty or fifty million bucks by summer.

But did he really want that kind of money? Did he want to become some huge drug kingpin who sold kilos of cocaine to gang leaders and drug dealers all over the Midwest? Did he really want to risk it all in hopes of getting the kind of money Bankroll Reese was playing with?

Absofuckinglutely.

He was ruminating about all that good drug money when his cell rattled against the birch veneer of the nightstand. Bubbles reached back, picked up the phone, and almost handed it to him until she saw the caller's name displayed on the screen. Her eyes became tight squints again, and they moved to Juice's.

"Kela? As in your ex-wife Shakela?"

"That's the only Kela I got in my phone." He reached for the iPhone, and Bubbles swung it around behind her back.

"Why the fuck is she calling you? Since when did this start?" Her tone was calm, inquisitive.

Juice thought, *Is it really any different from your rap superstar ex having your number and calling you whenever he wants to?* But he didn't say it. He didn't need to say it. Apparently, Bubbles had some psychic abilities she'd never told him about.

"I know what you're thinking," she said. "I have Blake's number saved in my phone and he calls me or whatever, but that's different. That's business. He's not my ex-husband, either. Here." She gave him the phone. "Don't make this a habit."

As if on cue, her iPhone began to ring just as he answered his, and she leaned back in a Matrix-like move to grab it.

"Juice, I need a favor," Shakela said immediately.

"What kinda favor?"

"Dawn said you don't have anybody living in that third-floor apartment on Drake. Would you mind letting me move in for a couple of weeks? Just until I can find me somewhere else to stay?"

"Are you fuckin' serious?"

"*Yes*, I'm serious. I can't stay another night with this crazy bitch. I don't know what the hell I was thinking moving in with her in the first place. Now she's fucking with this fat nigga across the street, swearing up and down she's only using him for his money. How can she be using him for his money when the nigga don't even got a job? She thinks he's *loaded* -- that's what she calls it when people have money, *loaded* -- but the nigga ain't got a pot to piss in and a window to throw it out of. He lives with his sister and her broke-ass boyfriend, and that old, dirty-ass Lexus he got is about to get repo'ed any day now."

"Wait a minute," Juice said, laughing. "You mean to tell me that you left your husband to be in a lesbian relationship with a woman who's now in a relationship with a man?"

"A broke man," Shakela elaborated.

Juice laughed again. "That's hilarious."

"It's really not. So can I use the apartment? If not, I can just stay with the twins."

"Can't you just get a hotel room?"

"Not when my daughter is pregnant. I'm staying close to her until she has our grandbaby. Come on, you can let me stay in your damn building. We got twenty years together, and—"

"Had twenty," he corrected.

"Listen, I know you got your li'l girlfriend. Okay? I'm not trying to get in between that. I got plenty of niggas checking for me. Fucking you is the last thing on my mind. All I need is a place to lay my head until I can find me somewhere nearby to rent. I'll be gone no later than the first of February."

Juice hesitated. "Okay, until the first of February," he said finally. "But that's it. No excuses."

"Don't do me," Shakela said, and he could hear the smile in her voice. "Thanks, Lee. I really do appreciate it. I knew you still loved me."

"Nah, nah, nah. Don't go too far. Shawnna got the keys. Go ahead and get yourself situated. I'll be over there in an hour or so." He ended the call before she could say anything else.

Bubbles was squinting down at him again, still holding her iPhone to her ear. She said, "Okay, let me call you back. Just stay in the house. I'll be out that way in a little while." Then she hung up and continued to stare at him.

"What?" he said

"What was all that all about? 'Shawnna got the keys.' What's that supposed to mean?"

He sat up and moved from beneath her, swinging his legs over the bedside. "I told her she could move into the third-floor apartment for a few weeks. I was about to rent it out anyway. It ain't no big deal."

Bubbles was in front of him in a flash. Hands on her hips, eyes burning holes in his face. It was obviously a big deal to her.

"Are you out of your mind?" She was leaning toward him, talking right in his face. "You're letting your ex-wife move into the same building you live in? Am I supposed to be okay with that?"

"If you don't trust me, that's on you. I ain't fucking with her like that. I was asked a favor by the mother of my kids and I said yes like any real man would have done under the same circumstances. She broke up with her girlfriend or something, and she needs a place to stay. That's all there is to it."

"That's all there is to it," she echoed, nodding her head slowly and deliberately.

He put his hands on her waist and pulled her closer to him. He kissed on the front of her shoulder, easing his hands around her thick butt to squeeze and rub. He knew his one chance at a good Christmas was making this beautiful woman believe she had nothing to worry about concerning him and his ex-wife being in close proximity to each other. Of course, he assumed that, sooner or later, Shakela would attempt to creep down to his first-floor apartment for a later night booty call, but he would deal with that later. One nightmare at a time.

"You're the only woman I wanna be with," he said, and planted a loud, smacky kiss on her lips. "I don't even wanna touch Shakela again. You hear me? *Ever*. All I want is you. Every day, every night. Every week, month, and year. All I want is Bubbles. So stop being insecure and jealous. Put some trust in me."

Her sexy brown eyes rolled up in their sockets. In one practiced motion he snapped off her bra - a white-lace Victoria's Secret number - and closed his mouth around a nipple.

"You think you're so slick, Juice." The anger in her voice had vanished, and now she spoke in a delicate whisper. "I can't stand your bald-headed ass."

He moved her panties to the side with one hooked finger and inserted a finger into her warm wet pussy. It seemed to suck his middle finger in deeper as she made her sex muscles contract around the probing finger.

"You might wanna wait until we make it back to your place for this," she said

"Why is that?" He slid his cigar into her, something he'd never done or even thought about doing before. She giggled softly and slapped him across the side of his head as he withdrew the cigar and put it between his teeth.

"Must you always be so nasty?" she said

"You said we should wait?" He lay back on the bed and looked down at the tent, his full erection made in his boxer shorts. "Tell him that."

"No, we absolutely *have* to leave," Bubbles reiterated. "I just got off the phone with Myesha. She just told Shawnna that they're both pregnant by Bankroll Reese, and now she's hiding at her next-door neighbor's house with a gun because she's afraid Shawnna might come over there and shoot her like she did Big Wanda."

Chapter 2

Rell and Tamera crashed through the front door, knocking over the wedding table that she had picked up at a luxury furniture store for eighteen hundred dollars. They hadn't spoken the entire car ride home from Northwestern Memorial Hospital. They had walked in silence up the front walkway that led to their porch stairs, him fuming, her unsmiling, and the jarring reality of Jah's condition weighing heavily on both of them. He'd swallowed down a pint of Hennessey to help deal with the pain. It hadn't helped much.

The moment she turned the key in the lock, he'd unfolded her gently in his arms and walked in, shouldering the door open and then kicking it shut. He kissed her eyes, her forehead, her salt-stained cheek, trying to comfort her while at the same time trying to comfort himself.

She tilted her head back, and he passionately mashed his lips against hers. She sighed, parted her mouth, and he found her tongue. He reached down and clenched her butt, and she responded by thrusting her pelvis forward and forcing it against his.

He hardened.

"I love you," he said, and they stumbled into the living room, banging into an end table as they went, not even bothering to turn on any lights.

She was peeling off her jeans and panties before they even made it to the sofa. Then her fingers were on his belt, unbuckling it, undoing the button on his jeans, yanking them down. They threw their coats on the floor, then added their sweaters to the pile.

The bedroom was too far away. He held her legs up in the air and entered her hard. She moaned involuntarily. The gripping pull of her pussy on his brick-hard pole helped take away the pain in his heart way more than the cognac. His pelvic area seemed to develop a mind of its own as he slammed his long phallus in and out of her. He kissed her again, more passionately than he had a moment ago.

He flipped her over, leaning her over the arm of the sofa and holding her waist in an iron grip. He couldn't remember ever fucking her so hard, not even on their honeymoon. Her moans were screaming moans. He wanted to stop and ask if he was hurting her, but he didn't want to stop. He didn't want to slow down. He had what felt like a ton of pent-up aggression boiling inside him. Big and round and impossibly soft, Tamera's buttocks slapped his pelvis with his every thrust.

"Yea, yes, yes, yes," she whispered, and he knew then that he wasn't hurting her - not unless she had suddenly become some kind of pain freak.

It was powerful, raw, it was pure, passionate, uninhibited healing sex. It was what he needed. What they both needed.

Somehow, she managed to get ahold of the TV remote, and she turned on their 75-inch UHD television and quickly muted the volume on the movie that was playing. In the light of the TV, they could see each other. He saw his dick, glistening with her juices, as he continued his ruthless assault on her tight pussy.

They had been going at it for more than thirty minutes when he rolled back over. He put both her legs over his left shoulder and gazed into her eyes, which were open just as wide as her mouth. She seemed to be in what he could only define as a blissful state of shock. Or maybe ecstasy was a better word for it. The expression was frozen on her stunning dark brown face, only shifting around the eyebrows when he went in deep.

Had he been eating her pussy, she would have climaxed a long time ago, but it took her longer to orgasm through penetration. He could sense it on the horizon. Tamera's pussy muscles squeezed his dick, and he held back until he heard the first familiar high-pitched moan. Her pitch grew louder and more frenzied, and he finally let go, stifling his own orgasmic sounds as he flooded her with his seed.

Her eyes glazed over. She slumped into his arms as he carried her to the bedroom. They stripped off the rest of their clothes and made love, slowly this time, gently.

When it was over, Tamera curled up in a fetal position and clutched a pillow to her chest. Rell wrapped his body around hers and pulled the blanket over them. He kissed the nape of her neck.

They shot my li'l brother, he thought.

"You going back up to the hospital tonight?" she asked.

"Yeah. After I get some rest. I'm still tired from last night. You can stay home this time. I'll go by myself."

"I'm going with you."

"Baby, you ain't gotta——"

"I'm coming whether you want me to or not," Tamera said sharply. "He's my husband's brother. That's my family too."

"He's your husband's brother and your sister's husband."

"That does sound a little weird, doesn't it?"

"Jerry, Jerry, Jerry!" Rell said drably. It was as if he was in a trance.

"Don't sound so down and discouraged. Jah's gonna be okay. He's a fighter. Look at all the things he went through late last year and earlier this year. He literally went to war with the whole 16th and Millard and came out on top, and he would've killed Zo if the police hadn't done it first. A few gunshot wounds won't kill that boy."

"I can't lose my brother," Rell murmured.

"You won't lose him. Stop saying that."

"The shit happened so fast. We had just stepped out the truck. I would've caught the pickup before it even pulled up, but I was watching Jah, making sure he didn't pull his strap on Juice."

"Why would he do that?"

"Because of what happened last night in L.A., the threesome Juice and Bubbles had with Tirzah. Tirzah got mad at him about something. I guess she told him about the threesome to piss him off."

"Well," Tamera said, "she lied if she said she had a threesome with Bubbles and Juice. She played with herself while she watched them fuck. I know you couldn't see over there with me riding your face." She snickered. "But that's what happened, I swear. She recorded some of it on her phone."

"So *that's* why she was looking so stressed out at the hospital. She knew that it was her lie that threw Jah off his square right when he needed to be focused."

It all made sense now. He had just been in the emergency room waiting area with Tirzah. She was wearing a little lipstick, but nothing else in the way of makeup, and her complexion had been a sickly shade of yellow-brown. There were dark brownish purple arcs under her eyes. It looked like she might have given her hair a token swipe with a brush before rushing to the hospital, but it hadn't done much good. It looked like straw and stuck out on either side of her head in a way that would have been Comic View funny under other circumstances. She'd been holding her iPhone up in front of her breasts, allowing him to note that the well-kept nails on that hand were gone. She'd chewed them off, right down to the quick.

"Your sister and my brother both need to go ahead and meet with some divorce attorneys," Rell said, but Tamera was already asleep, so he thought of a few different ways to go about learning the identity of the gunman who'd driven up in a black Dodge Ram and shot his eighteen-year-old brother five times.

An idea came to him a moment before he fell asleep, and he stored it away in the back of his mind.

King Rio

Chapter 3

"I'm about to squash this bug-bitch under my boots," Shawnna said through tightly-clenched teeth. She had one hand on the steering wheel of her smoke-gray Cadillac Escalade, the other on the Glock 23 pistol resting on her lap. She had on a black, White Sox hoodie over blue jeans and gray Timberland boots. In the passenger's seat, Dawn wore practically the same outfit, only her hoodie was gray and had a picture of Beyoncé throwing up two middle fingers printed on the front of it.

They had just turned onto 16th Street, and neither of them were surprised to see dozens of cars and trucks rumbling up and down the street. There were a bunch of Christmas Eve parties going down tonight. Lots of thirsty ho-ho-hoes looking to give the gift of high-mileage pussy to eager young men who would not hesitate to rip open those presents and play with them all night.

"Daddy just told us not to go over there fucking with that girl," Dawn said, drumming her fingertips on her knees. "He said she has a gun."

"So, the fuck what? I got one too," Shawnna said in a strangely calm tone of voice, and for the first time since they got in the SUV, her eyes met Dawn's.

"I'm just saying, Shawnna. Shit. If anybody's to be blamed here, it's the nigga you call your man. He's probably in New York giving another bitch a baby right now, and he got us out here about to stomp a bitch we've known since preschool. I'm with you - right or wrong, I'm riding with you till the wheels fall off - but I don't think we should be trying to fight Myesha over some nigga."

"It's not about Reese."

"Then what the fuck is it about?"

"She's supposed to be my friend. *That's* why I'm about to drag this bald-headed hoe all up and down Spaulding. Friends don't fuck each other's men."

"Keyword: *hoe*," Dawn said. "You and I both know that Myesha will drop it like it's hot for any nigga with a few dollars in his pocket. That's the main reason why she started stripping. And let's not forget that she works at *Reese's* strip club. Ain't no telling how long she's been fucking him."

Shawnna didn't say anything. She was focused on the road. It was snowing, but not a whole lot, just a steady sprinkle that flecked the windshield as they rolled forward, the traffic not allowing them to go any more than ten miles an hour at the moment. They passed Rev's Barber Shop and Supreme Hair, their salon, on the right, Tinky's Bar & Grill, and Redbone's Gentlemen's Club on the left. Tinky's looked packed, and so did Redbone's. Shawnna gave the strip club a nasty look.

"I should shoot that whole damn club up," she said finally.

Dawn laughed merrily. "You can't hate *all* the strippers."

"I'll shoot all them bitches." A smile played around the corners of Shawnna's mouth. "Myesha just fucked up my opinion on strippers. I'm ready to swing on the next stripper-bitch I see."

"All jokes aside. What are we about to do when we get to Myesha's house? Are you gonna try talking to her? Is it on-sight swinging? Let me know so I don't have to guess what happens next."

"I don't know," Shawnna said with a shrug. "We'll see when we get there. As a matter of fact, text that bitch and tell her to bring her trifling ass outside so we can talk face to face. Tell that hoe I got a gun too, so if she wanna get stupid, we can be two dead pregnant bitches."

Dawn chuckled once, not because she found humor in her sister's words, but because she knew Shawnna actually *meant* every word. That sort of crazy deserved a chuckle.

She began to type out a text message to Myesha, then changed her mind in the middle of the second sentence and dialed the number instead. It was answered at the start of the second ring.

"Myesha, can you——"

"This ain't Myesha," a gruff voice said, and Dawn knew right away that it was the man half the neighborhood knew as Detroit Lenny.

Like her father, Lenny was a big man. Burly, with thick cornrows and a mouthful of gold teeth. He could either be a welcoming presence or an intimidating one. Word on the street was he had fled Detroit after some Gangster Disciples he'd robbed had knocked on his mother's front door and shot her in the head when she opened it. Now he lived next door to Myesha on the 1500 block of Spaulding Avenue, a block that was ruled by Traveling Vice Lords and Four Corner Hustlers, all of whom worked for Juice.

"Is she around?" Dawn asked tentatively.

"Why?"

"Uhh, because I want to *talk* to her." She put it on speaker so Shawnna could hear.

"I hope y'all don't think I'm about to sit back and do nothin while y'all jump my girl. I can't let it go down like that."

Shawnna sucked her teeth. "Lenny," she said, and sighed. "Don't fuck around and get yourself fucked around, Lenny. Don't do it, Lenny. Stay in a man's place, Lenny. Because Shawnna Wilkins has been known to fuck a nigga up from time to time."

Dawn laughed. She couldn't help it.

"I'm not about to argue with no female," Lenny said.

"Good," Shawnna replied, "Because I don't wanna have to knock out no male."

"Ain't nobody gon' knock me out."

"Nigga, I'll knock your fat ass all the way back to Detroit. Like I said, stay in a man's place and tell Myesha to bring her ass outside to talk to me. I'll be pulling up in about thirty seconds. And you keep your penguin-built ass in the house, *Lenny.*" She looked at Dawn, who was laughing uncontrollably against the passenger door. "Bitch, hand up the phone."

Dawn slapped her knee with her left hand and ended the call with her right. She was shaking with laughter. God, her twin was hilarious. Mean as shit and prone to violence, but hilarious, nonetheless. She knew it was a bad time to be laughing - they were half a block from Spaulding Avenue and approaching fast - so she drew herself up and took a couple of deep breaths. "Oh my God," she said. "Shawnna, if you have us out here fighting Lenny's big ass, I am literally going to run the first time I get hit."

"Bitch," Shawnna said, picking up her .40-caliber Glock by its long 30-round magazine, "we got bullets for big niggas like him."

"Let's hope it doesn't come to that."

"It will if he walks up on me. You can believe that."

Shawnna made a hard left onto Spaulding Avenue. The street was lined with dozens of cars and SUVs, because one of those Christmas Eve parties was underway at one of the houses across the street from Myesha's house. With all the curbside spaces taken, Shawnna was left with no choice but to park in the middle of the street.

They didn't have to look for Myesha. She was standing on Lenny's front porch in a bright lime-green coat, hands in the pockets, shoulders pulled up around her ears. Lenny and another man were standing behind her.

"That's Lenny's brother standing with them," Dawn said. "I think his name's Marshall. He sent me a friend request on Facebook."

"Here," Shawnna said, and handed the Glock to Dawn. "Blast that bitch nigga Lenny *and* his brother if me and Myesha get to fighting and they try to jump in."

"Shawnna, you're pregnant."

"I wouldn't give a fuck if I was blind," Shawnna said. She shoved open her door and shouted, "Myesha, come over here and talk to me, so we can get an understanding about this shit."

Dawn put the gun in her purse, got out of the Escalade, and walked around to the driver's side as Shawnna stepped out in the street.

"I don't wanna fight you, Shawnna," Myesha said. "See, this is exactly why I didn't wanna tell you. I knew it would come to this."

"Come to what? Who said anything about a fight? I said let's talk." Shawnna was smiling like a fool. She put her hands in her hoodie pockets, twisting her upper body from left to right.

Reluctantly, Myesha came walking down the stairs. Lenny and Marshall walked her to the sidewalk and then let her walk alone into the street. She looked tense, afraid, and ready to take off running. She was the girl a lot of the guys in the neighborhood referred to as the "Chicago Amber Rose," because she was a light-skinned stripper with a big butt, a cute face, and hair that she kept cut very low and colored blonde. She was a bad bitch. Mostly everyone said she was the baddest stripper at Redbone's, although she hadn't danced there in a while. Her usually beaming smile was nowhere to be found.

She was stone-faced, trying to read through Shawnna's contemptuous smile.

"You tried to hurt me, didn't you?" Shawnna said.

"No, I didn't, no I didn't," Myesha protested, groaning inwardly. "You know how I am. I like to fuck. We turnt up one night and it just happened. I was drunk, he was off that lean and some pills. The shit just happened."

"The shit just happened," Shawnna echoed stiffly. She stuck out her bottom lip and nodded her head.

"I'm sorry it happened. I really am. You and Dawn have been like sisters to me since I was a little kid. I hope we're not about to let a man ruin all that history we have, because I can name at least ten other bitches Reese has been fucking."

Dawn leaned back against the Escalade, lifting the rubber heel of her boot and pressing it flat against the tire. She could hear the faint sound of contemporary rhythm and blues on the wind, drifting out of the Christmas Eve party. John Legend, maybe. Young black men and women listening to John Legend and drinking cognac, perhaps wearing festive Santa hats. Nice for them.

"I *love* y'all." Myesha looked briefly at Dawn, who nodded, and then back at Shawnna. "I never would have fucked him if I'd known you were going to be in a real-deal relationship with him. I was just having fun. It turned serious for a couple of weeks, but I fell back when I saw how much you and him were hanging out together. When he told me he loved you, I blocked his number out of my phone until I changed my number, around the time your daddy and Bubbles went to Vegas."

Shawnna nodded. "You gave us your new number and then ignored us. You stopped replying to our texts, stopped answering our calls. You stopped coming over. We haven't seen you anywhere."

"I couldn't come around you knowing I was pregnant by Reese," Myesha remarked, and then sighed. "If I would've let myself do some foul shit like that, I wouldn't have even been able to look myself in the mirror. It was actually my mom's idea to just stop all contact with you and Dawn. She said it would be more honorable to do it that way. She said, 'you don't wanna look like a snake when the grass gets cut.' So I took her advice and cut all ties to two of my best friends."

Just when it seemed like all was going well, Lenny stuck his chest out and came stomping toward the girls. "You ain't gotta explain yo'self to deez hoes! Look, you hoes bouta get beat up if y'all don't move around in the next two minutes. Think I'm bullshittin' if you want to."

"It's okay, Lenny!" Myesha said quickly, raising a hand, palm toward him.

"You bitch-made-ass nigga!" Shawnna said sharply. Her voice was high-pitched and replete with fire. "I hope you know you just bought yourself a one-way ticket back to Detroit, you bum bitch! Out here looking like DJ Khaled before he found the keys. Get'cho fake ass outta here. Nigga, you look like Rick Ross back when he was a C.O. with that cheap-ass fur on the collar of that coat. That's a squirrel tail. You squirrel-necked bitch."

It was hard for Dawn to keep a straight face, especially when Lenny's own brother began to chuckle. But Dawn stayed focused on Lenny, who was right behind Myesha, and on Marshall, who was now standing right at the curb. Lenny pointed an index finger at Shawnna's face, reaching over Myesha's shoulder.

"Stop *fuckin'* playin' with me, li'l girl," he barked.

"You played yourself, Bruce Bruce," Shawnna retorted snidely. "You're lucky my daddy even let your lame ass live in our hood this long. Out here looking like Big Yachty. Out here looking like Coolio in a fat suit. You big musty bitch. I should call the fashion police on yo' big bitch ass, 'cause yo' whole face stank. Bitch, you look like——"

Lenny's powerful left forearm swept Myesha aside as easily as a breath of air could move a falling snowflake. She went crashing to the ground elbow-first, while Lenny reached for Shawnna's throat.

Suddenly, Marshall came rushing at Dawn. Out of the corner of her eye, she saw Shawnna throw three quick punches at Lenny's face, but then her eyes were back on Marshall. Without a moment's hesitation, she whipped the gun out of her Fendi bag and aimed it at Marshall's head, but he got a hand on her right wrist just as she squeezed that trigger.

FOP! FOP! FOP!

He had her hands over her head. He rammed his forehead into her chin once, twice. Her vision got fuzzy around the edges. "Let go of the gun, bitch," he growled, and she thought he sounded like a homicidal bank robber, the kind who would make everybody lay face-down on the floor and then put a bullet in the back of someone's head just to prove he wasn't fucking around. He had the smell of ham on his breath. Maybe he'd just finished eating an early Christmas dinner and was good and full, ready to put a bullet in the front of her head to *really* prove he wasn't fucking around.

He was trying to pry the gun out of her hand.

She refused to let go of it.

She slammed her knee into his crotch. He doubled over in pain, and she threw her head forward. Her right eyebrow connected with Marshall's nose, and the animal noises coming from his throat were replaced by the sound of cartilage crunching and snapping. He stumbled backward, cupping his hands over his nose, his knees pressed tightly together.

Just as Dawn took aim and prepared to pull the trigger, Shawnna approached Marshall and punched him hard in the jaw. He went down like an empty laundry bag and didn't move.

"Oh my God," Dawn murmured. She looked to her left and saw that Lenny was also knocked out cold, lying on his back with his right arm straight up and his left arm out to the side, like a clock reading 12:15 or 3:00. "Oh my God, Shawnna. You knocked them out!"

"You're surprised?" Shawnna helped Myesha up. "I told you he was a big bitch. Him and his weak-ass brother." She smiled that contemptuous smile again, then uppercut Myesha on the chin.

It was knockout number three.

Shawnna grabbed Myesha's coat and carefully guided their unconscious friend to the ground, then opened the Escalade's driver door and got behind the wheel. Dawn returned to the passenger's seat, and Shawnna pulled off.

King Rio

Chapter 4

Bubbles adjusted the rearview mirror in her bone-white Mercedes Benz S550 to look at her twelve-year-old daughter. Ra'Mya had her head down, eyes glued to the screen of her iPhone.

"You okay back there, Mya?" Bubbles said.

"Yeah," Ra'Mya said, and her curly hair bounced as she nodded.

"What are you doing on that phone?"

"Watching mannequin challenges on YouTube."

"Don't be back there trying to text no boys. Percy's mom called and told me about what happened last night while I was in L.A."

"I didn't do anything wrong, Ma. He sent me a nasty pic and asked me to send him one. I was going to tell you, but you wasn't around at the time, so I told Shawnna. She took care of it."

"Percy's mom said Percy told her that some *boyfriend* of yours snatched him up and put a gun to his face. You got a boyfriend now?"

Ra'Mya giggled and shook her head. "I didn't have anything to do with that. You have to talk to Shawnna about that. She had Wayno come over and scare Percy for being nasty with me."

"You just make sure you don't text no more boys. And I mean *none*. One more situation like that and you won't touch another phone until you're my age. You got that?"

"Yes, Ma."

Juice chuckled. He was in the passenger's sent, smelling good (Mr. Burberry cologne she had gotten him) and dressed in a black-and-gold leather Monder jacket over a black Louis Vuitton sweater, Balmain jeans, and a simple brand-new pair of Air Force One sneakers - black like his Louis Vuitton skull-cap. She matched his fly in a white turtleneck sweater from Beyoncé's website (*I SLEIGH ALL DAY*, it read) over Prada pants and Gucci boots. Her high-end trench coat was pooled around her waist. Her lambskin Chanel bag was on Juice's lap. It was black to match her pants, boots, and fingernails.

"What are you laughing about over there?" Bubbles said. The red light turned green, and she applied pressure to the gas pedal, sending the long white Benz soaring up Kedzie.

"This text message I just got from Dawn," he said, tilting his iPhone so she could see the text. "We might as well just go on to the house. We're too late to save Myesha. According to Dawn, Shawnna just knocked out Myesha and two niggas who came outside with her."

"Oh my God, are you serious? Hand me my phone out that purse. God, I hope the baby's okay." She tried calling Myesha's phone, got no answer, and left a voicemail ("Girl, call me ASAP and tell me what's going on!"), and then re-garded Juice with her signature squint as she came up on another red light.

"What?" he said.

"You know damned well what. Myesha and I have been tight ever since the first day I walked into Redbones. Me and her go way back. I'm supposed to be that baby's godmother. What if she has a miscarriage over this?"

"You act like *I'm* the one who knocked her out."

"You might not've done it, but you're definitely responsible for it. It was you who raised that crazy-ass girl. Like father, like daughter."

"I don't think that's how the saying goes." Juice chuckled again. A small smile curved the sides of his mouth upward. "I'm surprised we're even driving back to my house. A few hours ago, you didn't wanna leave Lake Forest. The west side of Chicago was the most dangerous place in the world."

"That was before your ex-wife decided she wanted to move into *your* building on fu-fricking Christmas Eve. Like I'm some kinda dummy. Like I don't know what she's up to. I ain't slow."

"Why she gotta be up to something? How you know she ain't just in need of a place to stay?"

"Because I'm a woman, and I know how women think. She wants that old thing back. She misses her old boo."

Juice smile widened an inch. Bubbles glanced at him, saw the smile, and almost raised her fist to punch him on the shoulder until she remembered that it was his left shoulder that had the graze wound.

"Take that dumb smile off your face," Bubbles said. "I hope you know what's about to happen. Your ass is moving to Lake Forest with me. You might as well pack your bags as soon as we get in that apartment, because after tomorrow, you're not coming back to that building until she moves out."

"Yes, Massa."

"Think I'm playing all you want to."

"I know you're serious," Juice said, and put the cigar - the pussy-scented cigar - between the teeth on the left side of his mouth. "But you know I can't do that. Not with Shawnna being pregnant. Gotta be there for my baby girl. We'll just keep everything the same way it's been. Just me and you. Sometimes we'll stay at my place, sometimes we'll stay at yours. Shakela will be gone by the first of February. You won't even notice she's there."

Yeah right, Bubbles thought, pressing down on the gas again and propelling her S550 forward. The shadows had begun to fill Kedzie Avenue. Overhead, the sky was now purple. It might have been some distorting effect of the twilight, or her own paranoia exacerbated by the kush she and Juice had smoked before leaving her Lake Forest home, but there seemed to be people standing in every other shadow beneath the dark, looming buildings, watching her sparkling white luxury sedan as it floated past them. Even the building windows, caked with the dirt of decades - of centuries, perhaps - seemed to be staring at her. And it didn't help that some passing motorists snapped pictures of her in the middle of traffic, causing her to flinch several times when she mistook the flashes for muted gunfire.

The random picture-snapping was bound to go on for a while. Yesterday, her face had appeared on the Instagram pages of the most talked about celebrity couple in the country. First, she and her two friends -Tamera and Tirzah - had taken a pic with multi-platinum-selling, Grammy Award-winning rap artist Blake "Bulletface" King, and the rapper had posted the controversial photo on Instagram. It was controversial because Bulletface had cheated on his wife with Bubbles just over a year ago. The photo had sparked his multibillionaire wife's infamously short fuse, and she'd resorted to her old ways, firing a gun at the van he was in during an interview he'd had with *TMZ Live*. His wife - Alexus Castilla - had been arrested for illegally discharging a firearm and freed on bail a short while later. In a gesture of friendship that was clearly nothing but damage control, Alexus had invited Bubbles, Tamera, and Tirzah out to dinner at her Hollywood restaurant, which is how they'd ended up in a photo on Alexus Castilla's Instagram page. With Alexus and Bubbles combined 160 million Instagram followers, it was no surprise that people were recognizing Bubbles everywhere she went.

Bubbles consulted her interior workings and tickings and discovered she was in a state of slowly building terror. She felt as if her intestines had begun to crawl sluggishly around and around within her belly. Her mouth had a sharp unpleasant taste, almost as if she had unknowingly eaten a moldy slice of bread. She thought of all the Chicagoans who had been shot dead this year - over seven hundred of them, so far, at least that's what the news said - in notoriously gang-infested neighborhoods like North Lawndale and yet here she was, driving right into the thick of it, right into a goddamn war zone.

They were approaching Roosevelt Road. A green traffic light urged her forward. *Come on in*, it seemed to say. *Nothing to be afraid of here.* The suffocating hum of the traffic remained constant, not seeming to diminish, not seeming to grow any, either. It was like the constant push of the wind. Claustrophobia was beginning to nibble at her nerves. She felt they were being watched. She tried to dismiss the feeling and found that she couldn't. The shooting that had landed Jah in the hospital this morning played on her mind more and more, and finally she had to say something.

"Juice, do you ever worry about losing your life out here in these streets? I mean, you've already lost your son, and Cup and Lil Chally. Cicero Yayo, Ray Ray, Bay Bay, Jaws - so many people, you know? Do you ever worry that you might be next?"

He took the cigar out of his mouth, shaking his head. "Nah," he said. "Real niggas don't die." He sounded thoughtful, distant. "I don't wanna die, but I ain't scared to die. We all gotta go one day. I can't see myself ever being scared of going to a place where my son and my best friend are already at. You feel me? I can't be scared of that. If anything, I'm scared for my daughters. I'm scared I might not be there when they really need me one day. That's really my only fear. I'm ready for everything else." he returned the cigar to his mouth.

"Do you think you'll ever find out who shot at you all this morning?"

"Absofuckinglutely." Juice reclined his seat halfway back and lay there with his hands laced tightly together on his chest. "I feel for his ass when we do catch him. It's gon' be a scary sight for him and whoever's with him, I can guarantee you that. They think *Jah's* the wild one but wait until they see Rell in action. I remember the wild Rell, before he went to the joint. Shit, he was wild *in* the joint. I saw that same fire in his eyes at the hospital. He's the old Rell again. I had that same fire in my eyes when I found out they killed my son."

"Save same of that fire for me," Bubbles said, hoping the suggestive innuendo would break the tension she saw in his posture - the knuckles of his laced-together hands were in tight wrinkles, as if he feared they might disobey him unless he exerted a certain amount of pressure to keep them where they were - but he didn't laugh. He didn't even smile.

"I'm a little past the being-scared stage of life," he said, "but there is something that worries me." He paused, considering, then placed his cigar on top of her purse. "Of course, I'm not really much of a worrier. I pretty much just go with the flow, try to keep my mind on the cash flow, you know? But I'd be a liar if I said I didn't worry a little." He freed his left hand from the death grip his right had on it and held it up with the thumb and forefinger almost touching. "About this much."

"Well," Bubbles asked, "what is it that worries you?"

"That you might go back to Redbones' and meet another nigga with long money like I got, or maybe even longer money. That I might get jammed up in some kind of indictments and lose you, lose Dawn and Shawnna and everything I got. I know that might sound insane, but it's true. I be thinking that one day ol' boy - the billionaire rap star ex-boyfriend of yours - is gonna call and say he wants you back, and I don't know how you would respond to that. I can't name too many women who would say no to a billionaire." He scrubbed a hand down his face. "I really don't even feel right saying all this. I'm a street nigga. It's supposed to be money over bi- you know. The bro code, or whatever you wanna call it. But I guess I'm old school. I'm a fan of relationships, and I think you might leave me for a richer nigga one day. There, I said it."

He slid his hands together again and looked at her with defiance and uncertainty. Also, she thought, with some relief. He'd lain awake trying to imagine what it would be like to tell her that he feared she might one day leave him for a hustler with deeper pockets, and when he did it, she neither caught an eye-rolling attitude nor picked up her cell phone to call on any back-up men. Some men she'd dated imagined she had a collection of such men on speed-dial, just waiting to jump in and take their spot.

"Well, I can assure you that I will *never* leave your side unless we break up for some reason, and I don't see that happening. You're the only man I've brought around my daughter since I left her daddy in Gary. I'm happy with you. You're actually the best thing that's ever happened to me. I love you and you love me back, and that's the most beautiful thing to me. To be honest, I've been having some of the same worries. I keep thinking that one day you're gonna run into a new bad bitch and forget all about me. You just don't know how insecure I am about that. Half the girls at Redbones wanted you when we first got together. They really got thirsty when you pulled up in that Jaguar truck. You should've seen how geeked up all the girls got when they first heard about it. But I wanted you way before that. I've wanted you ever since I first saw you. And I hope this thing of ours never ends." She looked at him hopefully, then swung her eyes back to the road.

They were on 16th Street now. The sky was black, and a steady cold wind rattled some trash across the street and whipped at the jackets and scarves of the men and women going to and from their destinations. A police car had somebody in a blue Buick Regal pulled over on Christiana Avenue. A pair of teenage boys with dreadlocks were chasing behind four young ladies at the corner of Spalding Avenue and 16th Street. Two police SUVs were parked facing each other at the Currency Exchange on Homan, and they passed three more CPD squad cars before they made it down to Drake.

"A lot of police out here tonight," Bubbles said as she maneuvered her Mercedes into the space between the rear end of Shawnna's gray Escalade and the front end of Shakela's *red* Escalade. She thought about mentioning the family's obvious Cadillac fetish until the memory of Juice's son slumped over in a bullet-riddled red Cadillac on 16th Street resurfaced in her mind.

She turned toward her burly, incredibly handsome boyfriend, studied him calmly for a moment, and then turned to her window to see what he was looking at.

There was a black-on-black Dodge Challenger parked across the street. Its driver's window was down, and the white man in the driver's seat was holding a camera up in front of his face. It was one of those high-tech cameras, like a Nikon, and it didn't take the eyes of a genius to see that the man was taking pictures of Bubbles and Juice, and that he was a cop.

Chapter 5

"I gotta get Bubbles, Tamera, and Tirzah to host tonight at The Visionary Lounge," Bankroll Reese said, more to himself than to the three men seated around the table with him. They were on a Gulfstream Six private jet that had cost Reese over a hundred thousand dollars to rent for the day. Four Vice Lords. Balmain outfits, Louboutin sneakers, and hundreds of thousands of dollars' worth of gold and diamond jewelry gracing their necks, wrists, and pinkie fingers. The man sitting next to Reese was his uncle Kevin Earl, alias Kev (although, when you thought about it, it was really more of a name-shortening than an alias, but an alias, nonetheless), and just like his nephew, he held a Styrofoam cup full of lean - purple actavis syrup and sprite soda mixed together - in one hand, and a blunt stuffed with island sweet skunk kush in the other.

The two big men seated across the table from them were Chubb and Suwu. Chubb was dozing with his seat positioned flat like a bed. Suwu was sipping Hennessy out of a Styrofoam cup and gazing vacantly out his window as the jet soared through a pitch-black sky fifty thousand feet above ground. Before leaving NYC, the four gang members had dined at Baker & Co., a five-star Italian restaurant in the West Village, and they had pigged out on Cacio e Pepe Ma and Cheese and Bucatini with Swordfish. Chubb had enjoyed the eatery's signature dish so much that he'd had seconds.

It had been a celebratory dinner. After months of costly legal proceedings, Reese had finally been issued liquor licenses for the two new clubs he would be opening in New York in the coming months. One was a nightclub, the other a strip club. Red's and Redbone's Gentleman's Club, respectively. He was anxious to spread his wings, to dig his fingers into the packets of some hard-working New Yorkers.

And he was just as anxious to get back to Chicago. He had a slew of big-name recording artists performing at The Visionary Lounge tonight. The all-star roster of names included Young M.A., Kelly Rowland, Young Jeezy, Tip, Cardi B, and Juelz Santana. He'd shelled out more than a million dollars to get them all to spend Christmas Eve inside of his glitzy West Side nightclub, and now he had his sights set on three curvy women who'd unintentionally created a social media frenzy when they posed for a photo with Bulletface yesterday.

"I doubt if Tirzah will come," Suwu said, turning from his circular window to look at Reese. "She ain't leaving my li'l cousin's side." The little cousin he was referring to was Jahlil Owens. Jah and Rell were his cousins, and his sister, Tara, was Kev's wife.

"You might be able to get Tamera and Bubbles to show up," Kev said, and puffed on his blunt. "But I'm with Suwu on Tirzah. I don't think she's leaving that hospital. Tara said Tirzah been there all day with him. He just got out of surgery a couple hours ago. Doctors say he's fucked up, but he'll live. I know that recovery gon' be a bitch. It's been almost four months since I got hit up, and I'm still feeling that pain."

Reese nodded and sipped and puffed. The memory of that day in mid-September still haunted him. He remembered how his heart had swan-dived when Suwu phoned him with the news that Uncle Kev had been shot. Kev had taken two bullets to the back and two more to the leg, and if not for Suwu, he would have undoubtedly taken a bullet to the head. Suwu had paralyzed Kev's shooter with a bullet to the spine, effectively saving his brother-in-law's life.

"Everybody's talking about that damn picture," Reese said. His expression was serious; he was thinking hard. "All across social media, all you see is that same pic of them standing there with Bulletface. Either that one or the one of them at the table with Alexus. It's like they got famous overnight."

Suwu's nod suggested Reese was wasting time with the obvious. "Of course they got famous overnight. Alexus is the queen of the fucking world to black people. She's worth over eighty billion dollars. Anybody she's seen with gets famous overnight."

"I wish I could get her and Bulletface to show up," Reese muttered thoughtfully as he inhaled another puff of smoke. "They came the night I reopened the club, but they left not even ten minutes later."

"That's because Darren got killed in the parking lot that night," Suwu pointed out. "I was so glad when he finally got it. That nigga terrorized the hood. He killed Head and Lil Dave. He killed Junior and then turned around and robbed Juice. I heard it was him who whacked Shaila too." Suwu lay aslant in his spacious white leather seat, looking up at the ceiling. The muscles in the side of his face were working, and Reese knew he had something more to say. "Darren almost added me to his body count when Kev got hit up." He stopped, but it was only a pause; the muscles along his jaw were still flexing and relaxing. "When I started shooting at the nigga who shot Kev, Darren got to shooting at me." Another pause. "I could've been just as shot up as Kev was that day, or as Jah is today." Another pause. "Or dead like Junior."

"I don't really know a lot about Jah," Reese said, "but from what I've heard, he's a savage. Me and him went to the same high school. We ran in different circles, though you know I didn't really hang with nobody but Grindo and Lil Dave back then."

"That shit is really starting to fuck with my head," Suwu said, and he knocked his knuckles against his temple, as if he wanted to make sure Reese knew where his head was at. "My li'l cousin better make it. I feel for a nigga if he don't. I'm coming out of retirement if Jah don't make it. And that's on everything I love. I can't lose my li'l cousin. I raised that li'l nigga - him *and* Rell."

"He'll be good," Kev said, staring at his and Reese's reflection in the window next to his seat. Or maybe he was looking at the blinking red light on the backside of the phone's right wing. Reese wasn't sure. "Don't even let your mind wander down that road. Trust me, I'm just as sick of our people getting shot and killed in the streets of our city, but it's Chicago. It's been like that since before we was even thought of, and ain't shit we can do to change it. Only thing we can do is give the li'l homies some guns so they can change the score. The opps got one, we come back and get two. An eye for an eye, a life for a life."

"For real, though," Reese said. He leaned forward and flicked his blunt over the ashtray. "Can we get off this depressing-ass convo and get back to talking about the bitches? I'm tryna turn up with some bad bitches tonight. We got sexy-ass Cardi B at the club with *us* in about an hour. I'm tryna fuck her li'l ratchet ass."

"You need to be tryna turn up with some condoms," Kev said.

Reese jerked his head back and uttered a hollow, lonely laugh.

He knew Kev hated the fact that he had gotten Shawnna pregnant, and he supposed Uncle Kev kind of had a right to be upset. He was caught in the middle of the whole mess, and by no fault of his own. While Reese's mother and Kev shared the same mother, Kev's father, Jermaine Wilkins, was Juice's brother, which made him both Reese's uncle and Shawnna's cousin.

"I did fuck up," Reese admitted, "getting Shawnna and Myesha pregnant at the same time. They used to be best friends. I don't think they even talk no more. Myesha said something about getting out before the grass gets cut. Or something like that."

"I can't knock you for what you do, nephew. Just make sure you take care of Shawnna. Make sure her and that baby are good. That's all I ask."

"Unc, you know I love that crazy-ass girl. I tried to get her to move into the mansion with me. She said she ain't moving in unless I put a ring on her finger."

"You're too cool for that, huh?"

"I'm too *young* for that. I ain't even twenty yet. Plus, I got way too much money to be getting married. My daddy worked too hard to get all that money. I ain't about to let no woman take half of my bread when she decides she wants to leave me. Fuck that. I'll take care of her and the baby, but I refuse to look up five years from now and see her taking care of some other nigga with thirty million dollars of my money."

"That's why they have pre-nups," Kev said.

"Naahh. Fuck that. Maybe when I'm old like you, but not now."

"Old like me? I'm thirty years old. That's young."

Reese uttered another lonely laugh.

"All right," Kev said, and bared his teeth for a moment at the side of his Styrofoam cup. Not in aggression; it was, Reese decided, the expression of a man preparing to do some heavy lifting that would leave him aching the next day. "I don't know if I can express it properly while I'm high like this, but I'll do my best. The important thing to remember is that you need a real rider on your team, the kind that'll be there to help you heal up if you ever get shot like I did, or if you ever get sick or hurt in any way. You need a partner that'll hold you down and have your back through all the bullshit life throws at you. If you can't be faithful at this point in your life, let her know that. If you don't wanna get married right now, be up front with her and tell her how you feel. Be honest with her and let her be your rock. If not her, then find yourself *somebody* to love."

"It's definitely her," Reese said, stabbing his blunt out in the ashtray. "You see she's the only female I ever post pictures with. I just bought her that new Escalade, some earrings, and about fifty new pairs of shoes. I take good care of my girl."

"Yeah, but money ain't everything."

"I know that."

"Do you plan on telling her about Myesha's baby?"

"*Hell no.*"

"Why not?"

"Man, I'm not about to go through that shit. You know how crazy Shawnna is. And besides, Myesha saying it's Detroit Lenny's baby. For all I know, the baby might really be his. Or it might be somebody else's. She claims I'm the only nigga she was fucking, but you never know. She could just be putting the baby on me because I'm the only nigga she fucked who actually got some money. I want a DNA test for *both* babies, to tell you the truth."

Kev furrowed his brow. "So you think Shawnna was cheating too?"

"You never know," Reese said with a shrug. "We used protection every time until she got pregnant. Seems kinda funny to me."

Chapter 6

"I should knock your stupid ass out too," Shawnna said, glowering at Dawn as they once again sat at opposite ends of their living room sofa.

"What the hell did I do?" Dawn asked in a high-pitched tone of voice.

"You poked a hole in that condom, ol' dumb-ass bitch. Got me sitting here all pregnant and shit. Dumb slut."

Dawn gave an amused smile. Their mother was in the kitchen cooking dinner. The scrumptious smell of fried chicken and spaghetti drifted into the living room and made Dawn's mouth water. Mama would be staying the night in their apartment, moving into the one upstairs in the morning.

Shawnna had a towel-wrapped bag of ice balanced on the back of her right hand, and there seemed to be two more ice cubes behind her eyeballs. Dawn could see violence in these frigid eyes, a violence exacerbated by the rapidly fluctuating moods pregnancy evoked.

"Sorry about that," Dawn said, getting up. There was a crackling sound as she put her hands in the small of her back and stretched. "I'm going downstairs to talk to Daddy. Anything to get away from your evil ass."

"Call me evil again and see if I don't launch this goddamn ice-bag at your ugly ass face," Shawnna said, speaking at race-car speed.

"If I'm ugly, and you're my identical twin, then what does that make you? I'm curious to know——"

"It makes me the bitch that'll rearrange your whole goddamn face if you keep getting smart with me. So unless you wanna be turned into a Picasso painting for Christmas I suggest you get the fuck outta *my* face."

The threat sounded legit, so Dawn strolled out. In her periphery, she saw Shawnna looking after her with a mixture of anger and resentment. And just as she closed her fingers around the doorknob, she felt the bag of ice smack the left side of her face.

It was a hard, stinging smack that threw her head to the side so hard that the impact turned her legs into noodles. She crumpled to the floor, and the next thing she knew, Shawnna had her by the hair, whopping her in the face with a closed fist.

"Bitch…bitch…bitch!" Shawnna was speaking in a fierce whisper, murmuring an expletive with every punch she landed.

Dawn yelped "Agh!" a couple of times. "Maaa! Come… get this…crazy bitch…*OFF ME!*"

The loud, hard whops to the face continued. Dawn tried covering her face with her hands, and the punches went higher. She could almost feel the knots rising on her forehead as she became seven more bitches. It seemed like the skull-rocking whops would go on forever.

Then Mama came to her rescue.

She heard Mama running down the brief hall from the kitchen. "Shawnna! If you don't stop! Let her go! Let her go *now!*"

As soon as Dawn felt her hair get released from Shawnna's death grip, she turned her back to the closet next to the front door, scooted until her back was touching the closet door, and looked up just as another loud WHOP reverberated through the apartment.

Instinctively, Dawn flinched, but she quickly realized the last whop had not been a blow to her face, but a blow to Mama's jaw.

Mama collapsed to the hardwood floor, unconscious, left cheek on the floor, right cheek facing the ceiling. Her eyes were half-mast, and she was snoring.

This crazy bitch done KO'd our mama, Dawn thought as Shawnna left out the door. *I cannot believe this shit.* She didn't realize she was crying until she was hunched over Mama, trying to wake her up.

King Rio

Chapter 7

Juice had already been at the door when Shawnna came walking into the apartment with tears streaming down her angry face. She breezed past him with no explanation, and for a moment he just stood there in a state of confusion, wondering what in the world had just gone down in Shawnna and Dawn's apartment. Then he shut the door and went in search of Shawnna.

He found her in the dining room. There was a long table with a glass top. Around it were eight red maple chairs. Shawnna was just flopping down in the chair at the far end of the table.

Bubbles and Ra'Mya were in the kitchen, decorating a cake Juice had baked earlier this morning.

"What just happened up there?" he asked Shawnna.

"I didn't mean to do it." She sniffled and used the sleeves of her White Sox hoodie to wipe the tears from her face. Did you lock the door? Please lock it now if you didn't. I don't want Mama bursting in here ready to fight me when she comes to."

"When she comes to?"

"Just lock the door, Daddy."

Juice went to the door, locked it, and came back.

"It was an accident," Shawnna said.

"What was an accident?" Juice said.

"I was mad, okay? I was mad as you know what. I'm not even supposed to *be* pregnant. If Dawn hadn't poked a hole in the goddamn condom, I wouldn't even be going through this mess."

"Dawn poked a hole in the condom?"

"Yes. That's exactly what she did. She knew me and Reese were about to do what we do, and she poked a hole in the condom. It was the same day Junior got killed. She poked a hole in the condom so I could get pregnant by a rich nigga. I know how thirsty that sounds but it wasn't *me* that was thirsty. It was your stupid, ignorant, pea-brained daughter."

Juice pulled out the chair to the right of her and sat down. He leaned back, laced his fingers together on top of his head, and stared at her. "So, what happened up there?" he asked impatiently.

"I got in a fight with Dawn and Mama tried to stop me. I punched her in the face on accident. Knocked her out. I swear I didn't mean to do it. It just kinda happened. A reflex, I guess. I was just trying to get her off me."

"Were you trying to get Myesha and Lenny off you too?"

She looked at him blankly.

"Okay," he said, and shook his head. "You know Kela's about to go nuts, don't you? It's a good thing you're pregnant. If not for that baby in your stomach, she would beat your ass like she used to, and I wouldn't lift a finger to stop her. You're wrong, Shawnna. You don't hit your mother."

"I told you it was an accident. I was just so…" She sighed and blinked rapidly. She looked so much like her mother, only reddish-brown instead of dark brown, and with a thinner nose. "I was pissed off, Daddy. I was pissed off and I guess I kind of blacked out. I don't know. This pregnancy is driving me crazy. And it's all Dawn's fault."

"Have you talked to Reese since you found out he might be Myesha's baby's father?"

Shawnna shook her head, and a fresh burst of tears went trickling down her cheeks. "His phone's on airplane mode. He's supposed to be coming right over here." She sniffled and balled up her fists, both of which were bruised and swollen.

"That dirty son of a bitch. Excuse my language. I could strangle that boy right now. I just fell out with Myesha because of him. You *know* how much I love her, Daddy. You *know*."

She began to cry. Juice leaned forward and put a hand on her knee. His heart ached for Shawnna. Although she was technically an adult now, she was still his baby. Always would be.

Momentarily, the impromptu photo shoot he and Bubbles had experienced at the hands of Chicago's finest receded to the back of his mind. It hadn't lasted long - just four or five headshots, and then the black Challenger had driven away - but it had been enough to put him on edge, to get him wondering if he might be caught up in some state or federal investigation. His biggest fear was being taken away from his family again. He'd been sitting in the same chair Shawnna was sitting in now ever since he walked in the door, worrying that his days of freedom might be numbered, when he heard thumps and screams coming from the apartment on top of his.

"Baby girl," he said, gently squeezing her knee, "don't let life beat you. Stop using your fists all the time. Start using your mind. Now when Reese pulls up, I don't wanna see you acting like you belong in a mental hospital. I raised you way better than that. You owe Myesha an apology, you owe Dawn and——"

"No. Not Dawn. Myesha and Mama, maybe, but not Dawn. She actually deserved what I gave her ass." Another sniffle. "But you're right. I stepped out of character. My hormones are all over the place and I haven't been myself lately. I got this." She drew herself up, sleeved her face dry, and - slowly, wincing - unballed her plump fists. "I know how to play this game. I'm done getting mad. It's time to start playing the same game."

"Whatever you do," Juice said, leaning in to get a closer look at a scratch on the side of Shawnna's neck, "just make sure you keep that baby safe. You're gambling with the baby's life every time you fight somebody while you're pregnant. What's this scratch on your neck?"

"That nigga Lenny tried to choke me. I knocked his big ass out soon's he got his hand around my neck. Mike Tysoned his punk ass. You should see the bruise his brother left on Dawn's chin from head-butting her when he was trying to take my gun from her. I knocked him out too. I really was about to let Myesha slide until Lenny and his brother attacked us."

Juice nodded. He was gritting his teeth. He took out his phone and dialed the number to his right-hand man (who had ironically taken a bullet to the right wrist this morning). It rang twice, and then Wayno answered.

"*Man*," Wayno said, "I know you heard about what Shawnna just did over there on Spaulding. They say she knocked everybody out."

"They put their hands on my daughters," Juice said tightly.

"Is it a green light?"

"They put their hands on my daughters," Juice repeated coldly.

"Say no more. They got a thousand police riding around out here right now, though. We can't even make a move. I'm posted up at Tamia's apartment. Want me to send Lil Mark over that way? You know he don't give a fuck. He'll hit a nigga up right in front of the police."

"Just have somebody keep an eye on Lenny's spot for now. I don't need another situation like what happened this morning. When the cops leave, bring the Glocks out. And take them somewhere else. I don't want no more shootings in North Lawndale for at least the next two weeks. I just had two pigs parked across the street taking pictures of me and my girl when we pulled up. I don't know what the fuck that means, but it can't be good."

Shawnna's eyes got wide. She brought a hand up over her mouth and gasped, and Juice thought she might be thinking back to that dark morning eight years ago when the Chicago Police Department busted through their front door and took her father away for seven long heart-wrenching years.

"Damn, for real?" Wayno said.

"Yeah," Juice said. "Two white cops in a black car."

"A black Challenger?"

"Yeah."

"That's Bryant and Milam. They work homicides. Bryant is the same cop that killed Zo. Remember that? It was all over the news. I think he switched over to homicide after he got cleared from Zo's murder. They pulled me over twice last week. Wrote me up on a bogus speeding ticket. I don't trust the one with the blonde hair. He acts like he hates black people. He might've just been taking pictures of the front of your building because of what happened this morning."

"No," Juice said, getting up. "He was definitely taking pictures of me."

"Shit," Wayno said. "Then I'd be worried."

King Rio

Chapter 8

Sleek and new and exorbitantly priced, the Bentley Bentayga was officially the fastest SUV on the market. The one Bankroll Reese owned was - as far as he knew - the only one on the streets of Chicago. He'd recently gotten all his vehicles painted a bloody shade of red, and the exterior paint on his Bentley SUV matched its soft lambskin seats.

He usually let Chubb or Suwu drive, but Suwu had gone to the hospital to be with Jah, and Chubb had gone home to spend the rest of Christmas Eve with his wife and kids. So it was just him in the Bentley Bentayga when he pulled up in front of Juice's building on Drake Avenue, and Uncle Kev was following behind him in a blood-red year-old Bentley Mulsanne.

He laid on the horn and looked up at the second-floor windows. He had sent a text message to Shawnna letting her know he was on 16th Street two minutes ago. She'd read it. So where was she?

He pulled over across the street from the building, picked up his iPhone from the center console, and was just about to dial Shawnna's number when she came strolling out the door in a black hooded sweater, jeans, and Timbs. He smiled at her sexy, unsmiling face as she got in next to him.

"Hurry up and pull off," she said morosely.

"What's wrong with you, baby?" he said, brows knitted.

"Just drive before my mom comes out here."

"Juice and Kela got back together?"

"No. She's in my apart——"

"Is Bubbles in there?" Reese said, and he was already dialing Bubbles' cell phone number. "I'm tryna get her and Tamera to host tonight." The call went straight to voicemail.

"She's staying in with my daddy. Can you please drive the fuck off? Or are you just going to ignore me?"

Reese cracked a grin. He dropped the transmission into drive and cruised off from the curb. Keeping his eyes on the road, he leaned over the center console and with a loud smack kissed her left cheek. Her perfume lingered in his nose. Her hair was long, black, and straight except for the blonde ends that curled upward. Her eyes were stuck to the windshield. She hadn't looked at him since she got in the passenger's seat.

"You're the sexiest girlfriend I've ever had, you know that?" he said, making a slow right turn onto 16th Street. "I had a nice long talk with Kev on the flight here. A talk about us. Me and you."

"Hmm." Her eyeballs rolled up in their sockets and then rolled back down to the windshield.

"I want you to know that I really do love you, Shawnna. And that's on my father's grave. I might not always…make the best decisions. But you're my queen. I want you by my side through it all."

She began to nod her head, her sexy pink bottom lip poked out. Ahead on 16th Street, there were several CPD vehicles parked on both sides of the street. One of them had a yellow mustang pulled over in front of his strip club. Although he had a Styrofoam full of Lean in his cup holder, a blunt in the ashtray, and a Glock on his lap, Reese wasn't paranoid. If he got arrested, he'd be out in a matter of minutes. It would be nothing more than an inconvenience, a minor one, at that. And besides, he figured, it was much better to be caught with the .45 caliber Glock on his lap then to be caught without it. The 30-round clip sticking up out of Shawnna's Hermès bag told him she felt the same way.

"Why you ain't talking to me?" he said.

"I'm listening," she replied.

"You wanna stop by the mansion and put on one of your dresses? Maybe a fur coat and some diamonds? I want you to be my date to the biggest event in the city tonight. I got Jeezy in the building. I got Tip in the building. You ready to fuck the club up with me?"

She shrugged indifferently. "Sure, I'll go."

"Why am I getting the feeling that you're mad at me for some reason? Did I do something wrong?"

"I don't know." She looked at him finally. "Did you?"

She knows about Myesha, Reese thought immediately. *Shit*. He thought of that scene from *Menace to Society*, when the big bald-headed black cop told Caine, "You know you done fucked up, right?"

His iPhone rang, saving him from having to answer her question - for now, at least. It was Kev calling. He put the phone to his ear as he made an easy right onto Homan Avenue.

"What's up, Unc?" he said.

"We're being followed," Kev said. "A white Explorer. It followed us off Drake."

"A white Explorer?" Reese said, and reached up to shift the rearview mirror.

Shawnna whipped around in her seat. "Detroit Lenny," she said in an urgent whisper.

"Detroit Lenny?" Reese said, looking at the white Explorer in the rearview mirror. He put the iPhone on his lap, turned on the speakerphone, and picked up his gun. "Why in the fuck would he be following us?"

"Because I knocked him out, I knocked his brother out, and I knocked his girlfriend out," Shawnna said, grabbing her own Glock in a manicured hand that Reese now noticed was terribly swollen. She stared at him for a brief moment. "I'd like to give a huge thanks to you for that whole situation." Then her eyes were back on the white Explorer, which was two car-lengths behind Kev's car. "He's probably waiting to get away from all the cops on 16th Street. I hope he's not thinking what I think he's thinking."

"Let him think it," Reese said, lowering his window.

Cold air swept into the Bentayga. Shawnna pulled the hood of her sweater over her head and yanked down on the strings, tightening the hood around her face. She pushed a button that opened the sunroof as they passed 18th Street. Snowflakes sprinkled in from the dark sky above.

"Want me to get him out the way?" Kev said

"Nah, not right now. Be ready, though," Reese said.

And then it happened.

The Explorer veered left, into the northbound lane of oncoming traffic, and raced forward. Heart pounding erratically in his chest, Reese rested the tip of his gun barrel on the window ledge and prepared for the inevitable. He heard Kev shout a warning, heard himself tell Kev to shoot. He felt movement on the right of him, and then there were gunshots, so many gunshots that he couldn't count them. In his sideview mirror, he saw that the bullets were stitching across the Explorer's windshield.

Just as the Explorer swerved left and slammed into the driver's door of a parked minivan, Reese stomped on the gas pedal. Some part of his mind knew that it was Shawnna firing the shots, but it didn't fully register until he glanced over and saw her slither down from the sunroof with the smoking gun in her hand.

Chapter 9

Juice's bedroom was a dark and sterile box featuring a stringently neat king bed and a 70-inch TV. The counterpane of the bed was turned back in a neat triangle, ready to admit the owner to the comfort of fresh sheets after a hard day's work. There was a desk with nothing on it but a Dell PC hooded with a transparent plastic dust cover. The floor was plain oak planks. There were Chicago Bulls rugs on either side of the bed. There were old pictures of his children on the wall. The single big window was curtained, and it also had blinds, which admitted a few dull spokes of light from the neighbor's Christmas decorations. The light blue curtains matched the walls and made the room look less skeletal than the others.

He was sitting at the desk, ruminating about the homicide detective taking his picture. Bubbles was in the kitchen cooking a quick dinner of burgers and fries. She had a Solange song playing so loud he could hardly hear himself think, but he didn't mind the sounds. He had a bottle of Budweiser in one hand and his iPhone in the other. The TV was on but he wasn't watching it.

"Step-daddy," Ra'Mya said as she stuck her head into the room, "my mom wanna know what all you want on your burgers."

"Two slices of cheese…let's see, uhhh…ketchup, mustard, and pickles."

"Yuck."

"Don't 'yuck' my sandwich. You got my sandwich yucked up."

She dropped her head back and laughed. "Ma, your boyfriend got problems," she shouted, looking and sounding like a twelve-year-old version of her ma.

"Grab me another beer too," Juice said as she headed back to the kitchen.

He leaned back in the desk chair and smiled to himself. Ra'Mya had a way of bringing that smile out of him. Such a sweet kid, she was. He hadn't been around his own daughters when they were her age. He'd gone to prison when the twins were ten years old and by the time he came home, they were seventeen. He realized with Ra'Mya that he'd missed some of the best years. Bubbles was a great mother who'd done an excellent job at raising an intelligent little lady.

The iPhone lit up in Juice's hand, and he saw his ex-wife's name flash on the screen. Below that were two options. One green, one red: accept, decline.

He considered pressing decline.

Don't call me, he thought, *call your girlfriend. The girlfriend you divorced me for.*

But he shoveled the grudge aside and accepted the call.

"You tell that bitch," Shakela started, "*I* said … if she brings her funky ass through this door again, her ass is grass and I'm a lawnmower. The kind you ride on, because I am most certainly going to ride *all over* her ass. Do you know that slut had the nerve to sucker-punch me? I was trying to get her off Dawn, and she spun around and fucking sucker-punched me! She's about to have that baby five months early, because I'm kicking it out of her ass tonight. Let her walk through this door. Tell her to bring her ass back up here if she's fucking froggy, because I'm Queen Kermit up in this bitch tonight!"

Juice was laughing silently up until the Queen Kermit part. Then he laughed out loud. He couldn't help it. You could have put a gun to his head and he still wouldn't have been able to help it.

"Oh," Shakela said, "so you find this shit funny?"

"No," Juice said, "I find the shit that's coming out your mouth funny."

"You find it funny that your daughter assaulted her mother? Really? You really find that shit fu——"

Juice ended the call abruptly. "Ain't nobody tryna hear that shit," he muttered aloud to himself. "Call and cry to your girlfriend. Juice got other fish to fry."

She called back just as Ra'Mya came prancing into the bedroom with his beer in one hand and his plate balanced on the palm of her other hand. He declined the call and accepted the food and beer.

"There you go, Big Nasty," Ra'Mya said, and put her hands on her hips. She wore an ear-to-ear smile and a neck-to-ankle pair of flannel pajamas.

"My name ain't Big Nasty, Lil Jerk," Juice said with a chuckle.

"And my name ain't Lil Jerk, Big Nasty." Her smile morphed into an expression of utter disgust as he took a big bite out of one of his two burgers. She shook her head slowly. "You're nasty for two reasons." She held up two fingers, forefinger and middle. "For one, you eat mustard. That alone pretty much lets me know you'll eat anything. Nobody in their right mind eats mustard. I don't eat it, my mom doesn't eat it, my *grand*mom doesn't eat it. Yuck. Just plain nasty."

Juice chuckled and chewed, chuckled and chewed. His phone vibrated on his knee; a text message alert, probably from Shakela.

"And for *two*," Ra'Mya went on, "you drink *beer*. With your *food*. Capital Y, capital U, capital C, capital K. That's what that is. Yuck in all caps. You're like Jessica Steinway; you'll put anything in your mouth."

"Whoa, whoa, whoa, whoa, whoa," Juice said. "Don't compare me to no girl. I don't know who she is and I really don't care to know. I'm a man, not a——"

"Jessica Steinway is the girl at my school who let all the eighth graders put their wee-wee in her mouth."

Juice spun around, sat his plate and beer down on the desk, and got up. By the time his legs were straight, Ra'Mya was already out of the room, repeatedly screaming "Ma!" as she sprinted for the kitchen.

When he made it into the kitchen, the mother and daughter duo were both laughing heartily. Ra'Mya was behind Bubbles, arms wrapped around her mom's chest. Her mom was holding a steel spatula, greasy with the brownish juices of fried ground beef patties. She pointed it at Juice in a threatening manner.

"Back away from my baby, Juice," Bubbles said.

"Nuh-uh. Fuck that. You know what she just said to me?" He moved toward them.

"Ma!" Ra'Mya screamed.

Juice peeled her off her mother and held her upside down by her ankles. He turned and started back down the hall, while Bubbles went back to the stove.

"Let my baby go, Juice," Bubbles said

"You want me to let her go?" he said as he turned into the laundry room.

The washing machine was a top loader, its hatch open. A box of Tide stood on the shelf next to it. Juice held Ra'Mya up over the hatch.

"I'll let her go right now," he said.

"No!" Ra'Mya shouted, laughing.

"Apologize."

"I'm sorry, I'm sorry! Put me down!"

He put her down on her feet and playfully shoved the back of her head as she took off for the kitchen again.

Five minutes later, the three of them sat at the dining room table and bowed their heads in prayer ("God," Ra'Mya said, "please forgive Big Nasty for drinking beer and eating mustard." Then "ouch!" as Juice squeezed her hand). When they were done eating, they went to Juice's bedroom, shut off the lights, and Bubbles turned on a Tyler Perry movie. Ra'Mya sat at the foot of the bed, while Juice and Bubbles sat up against the headboard.

About five minutes into the film, Ra'Mya got a phone call and rushed off to her bedroom (she'd over the past few months customized the guest room and claimed it as her own).

"Let me see..." Bubbles picked up her own iPhone from the bed-table, thumbed her way to an app, and read something. "Oh, it's just her friend from school."

"You spying on her?" Juice said

"I'm *parenting*," Bubbles said. "Get it right. There are way too many strange people in this city. You heard what happened while we were away in Los Angeles yesterday. Now I got some little boy's mom mad at me because he sent a pic of his little wee-wee to my daughter's phone."

"I think she might be mad that Shawnna picked him up for a movie date and set him up to get pistol-whipped and threatened."

"Shawnna is my kinda girl. I might not agree with her putting her hands on Myesha, but what she did to Percy made me Team Shawnna all day every day. She can't do no wrong in my book."

"Not even if she knocked her mama out?"

"*Especially* if she knocked her mama out. That's what Kela gets for coming over here in the first place. Got me looking all ratchet living in a building with my man and his ex-wife when I got a whole house I paid damn near $2 million for in Lake Forest."

Juice slapped a hand on her big soft butt as she got out of bed. She went to the closet. She did have a point. Her Lake Forest home was huge, so incredibly massive that the master bedroom had two walk-in closets, the basement had a kitchen area, a dance studio, and an art studio, and the property had its own stretch of forest preserve that guaranteed a dear sighting every day or so if you looked long enough.

"This little-ass closet," Bubbles complained bitterly as she came out of it with a large plastic bag that he hadn't even known was in there. "You need to rent this place out and just move in with me. If you want the twins close to us so bad, then get them a place out there. The rent's about three grand a month. You can afford it. As a matter of fact, I'm almost positive Shawnna can get Reese to pay the rent. All you have to do is get them moved in."

"What's in the bag?" Juice asked

"A bigger closet," she said smartly. Strolling toward the bedroom door, she glanced back at the computer desk. He'd left his smartphone there, and now its glass screen was lighting up. "I thought we were turning off our phones for the night?"

"That's my bad."

"It better be off when I get back." She left and padded up the hall.

Juice got up and grabbed his cell phone. This time it was Dawn calling. He sat down at the desk and answered it.

"Mom's pissed at you," Dawn said immediately.

"That ain't none of my concern. Are *you* okay? And what's this talk about you poking a hole in a condom? Did you really do that?"

"I'm fine. I thought my face would be all knotted up, but she was hitting me with her right hand - that's the one she messed up fighting Myesha, Lenny, and Marshall - so it didn't do much damage to me. Just busted my nose and the inside of my cheek. She hit mama with that *left*, though. Jesus Christ. Is she still down there?"

"Nah. Reese came and got her."

"Good. She should stay with him tonight. Mom's on fifty."

"Did you poke a hole in her condoms?"

A guilty sigh blew through the phone.

"I take that as a yes," Juice said

"It was dumb, I know. A really dumb move. It seemed like a good idea at the time, but it was the wrong thing to do. I see that now. You don't have to get on me about it. My head's already throbbing from the beat-down I just took for doing it. I'm lucky I didn't get knocked out too."

Juice laughed. "Shawnna went on a spree tonight, didn't she?"

"It ain't funny, Daddy."

"The hell it ain't. Y'all better quit messing with my baby while she's pregnant. I think she's done playing games."

"You mind if I ask you something?"

"Something like what?" Juice was gazing vacantly at the TV. Madea and the woman who'd played Craig's mom in *Friday* were in some kind of shopping mall. Juice hadn't seen this movie before.

"You got to meet Alexus and Bulletface yesterday," Dawn said. "You know I have a million and one questions."

"Ask away. But I'm letting you know right now, when Bubbles comes back into this bedroom, I'm hanging up."

"There's a rumor floating around on social media that's basically saying Alexus got mad at Bulletface for taking the picture with Bubbles because she really wants to get back with T-Walk. You know who T-Walk is, right? He's like a black Ryan Seacrest. He produced a bunch of hit TV shows, including the one his girlfriend Thunder is on. But anyway, they thought T-Walk was dead, turns out he isn't and I wanna know if you or Bubbles heard anything about it. I mean, I know Bubbles knows *something*. She *did* have dinner with the *queen*."

"So, what's the question?" Juice chuckled.

"Did Alexus say anything about T-Walk?"

"I didn't really talk to her. You'll have to ask Bubbles about that."

"What did you and Bulletface talk about?"

Kilograms of cocaine, Juice thought with a smirk. *We talked about him giving me a thousand kilograms of cocaine for $10 million.* But of course, he couldn't say that.

"A little bit of this," he said, "a little bit of that. We talked about Cup and Lil Cholly. I told him that Cup's son was my daughter's boyfriend now."

"Hmm. And who else's?" The shade in Dawn's tone of voice was palpable.

"We talked about me and Bubbles," Juice sailed on. "He wished us well. That was about it. After that he invited us to come backstage with him and all the Money Bagz rap artists … at the D Boy and Deja concert. And we kicked it on the tour bus with him and Biggs. He paid for us a suite at the Four Seasons in Hollywood. We had a good time."

"I am soooo jealous. I would literally kill to sit at the same table as Alexus. Did you know that she took Bill Gates's spot as the number-one richest person in the world last month? She's worth over eighty-two *billion* dollars! I swear, if I could just meet her and Beyoncé, I would never want another thing in my life. I would die a happy won -" She stopped talking and gasped. "Do you think…?"

"Do I think what?" Juice said, leaning back in the chair and stretching his long legs out in front of him.

"Remember a while back when Alexus and her family were under investigation for being involved with a Mexican drug Cartel?" Dawn's voice was low, almost a whisper. Conspiratorial. "Do you think that maybe some of that money she has came from some kind of drug cartel?"

King Rio

Chapter 10

Jose Padilla was having a hard time piecing together the chain of events that had transpired from about 8:30 p.m. until now, mainly because his feet were nailed to the floor and a foul-smelling bag was pulled down over his head. It was kind of hard to think clearly under these conditions.

His afternoon had started off slightly different than usual, but only because it was Christmas Eve and he had an American supermodel girlfriend he'd wanted to impress. He had spent well over two hundred thousand dollars on the girlfriend - Heather Rasby, a fine London-born twenty-year-old who resided in a posh Beverly Hills high-rise when she wasn't here in Mexico with him - to make this the most special Christmas she'd ever experienced.

He had taken her out shopping in Mexico City, the two of them traveling from store to store in the back seat of his snow-white Range Rover while three more identical Rovers tailed them, both of them snorting coke and drinking Cristal champagne and chain-smoking cigarettes.

"You live like an A-lister," Heather had said when they were sauntering through the Gucci store, "yet none of the girls I hang out with have even heard of you."

"International man of mystery," he'd replied wittily.

And he *was* a man of mystery. He was the co-founder of the newest drug cartel in northern Mexico - the Padilla-Chavez Cartel, according to the DEA's televised statement following a drug bust this past July. The bust had taken down forty-eight members of the cartel, some of them high-ranking. It had been a devastating blow to the drug cartel's operations, but it wasn't enough to render the cartel inoperable. There were now more than two thousand members of the Padilla-

Chavez Cartel, many of them former members of the Matamoros Cartel, and it had only taken a few meetings between the founders - Jose Padilla and Julio Chavez - and their underbosses to refill those forty-eight positions.

Padilla was a millionaire several times over. So was Chavez. The two men had defected from the Matamoros Cartel after learning that the drug money was being used to finance Alexus Costilla's television network, and it had been easy to get a thousand others to leave with them.

At around six this afternoon, Jose Padilla had returned home to his Juarez City compound with his supermodel girlfriend and seventeen armed soldiers. Thirteen more heavily-armed men had already been patrolling the compound, so Jose had felt comfortable as he and Heather retired to the master bedroom, where they had loved each other in eight different positions until the blood of sunset was replaced by the cool gray ashes of twilight.

It was approaching 8:30 when he dozed off, and now here he was, bound to a chair with a bag over his head and his feet nailed to the floor. He'd already been bound to the chair with the bag over his head when he came to, but the nails in his feet had only been there for two or three minutes, five at the most. He had heard the nail gun. He had screamed and groaned, and he was still groaning a little. It was a low, sobbing groan.

The pain was excruciating.

He'd been drugged. He knew that much. There was no way he could have been put in this chair without waking up unless he was drugged. Had he been taken to a different location? Was he still in his bedroom? He didn't know.

In Spanish, he bellowed, "Goddammit, what do you want? You want pesos? I got pesos. You want dollars? I got dollars! *Millions* of dollars! Release me and I'll give you five million, no questions asked. Just give me half an hour. Let me go and give me a half hour and I'll give you five million dollars."

The response he got wasn't human.

Moooooo.

He angled his ear toward the sound. "A *cow?*" he murmured in disbelief. "A fucking *cow?*"

There came another long moo. This one seemed closer, right in front of him. Was he in a barn? Had someone brought a fucking *cow* into his compound? And where was Heather? Was she okay? Was she nailed to the floor in another room? God, he hoped not. Heather was such a sweet girl. He hoped she was okay.

He heard a noise behind him. A footfall.

The bag came off his head, and he found himself staring at the back end of a cow. He was duct-taped to a chair in a big warehouse filled with terrible steel objects: tables, saws, sharp hooks rotating around on a big machine. It was a slaughterhouse, he realized, and there were naked men hanging from some of those hooks. About thirty men.

His men.

Standing next to the cow was a tall, slender man in khaki shorts, an old yellow golf shirt. The overhead fluorescent fixtures sent down a merciless light, and Jose could see the deepening crow's-foot at the corner of his eye, the smattering of gray along the side of his short haircut. Jose put him at about fifty. He was typing something on a smartphone.

He snapped his head around. There was an animal quickness to him that made Jose's stomach sink. His eyes were of a blue much more vivid than Heather Rasby's. Jose saw nothing in them he recognized as sanity, and his heart sank further. On the floor - the same shimmering steel as the rest of the slaughterhouse, dark with bloody footprints - there was an assault rifle with a rifle scope on top of it.

"I'm Francisco," the blue-eyed man said. "I'm the new guy around these parts. You're the new guy, I'm the new guy. We should start a band. We could be The New Guys." He seemed to consider this, and while he did, he patted the cow on the belly. "I know we haven't met, but you may have heard of my father. He was legendary in the drug-trafficking business. He just about ran Mexico until the Zetas cut off his head. His name was Segovia. Ever heard of him? Segovia Costilla?"

Jose peeled his lips back from his teeth in a seething snarl. "You're no fucking Costilla. Who are you? What do you want from me?" Glancing down at his feet, he saw that the chair he was bound to was elevated on top of a foot-high wooden platform. The nails were sending long, rippling waves of pain up his legs. He was in his boxers, nothing else.

"Oh, I'm a Costilla," Francisco said. "It's just that my brothers and I were illegitimate, you know? You know. I'm sure you know all about cheating husbands. You're one yourself. I know that. You and I both know that. The New Guys know that." He laughed. Two quick yips. "Okay, the chase. I'll cut to it. I'll cut right down to the chase. Papi? You know Papi. I never got to meet my brother. Papi and Flake *were* my brothers, you know? You know. Okay, maybe you don't. But my *niece*. You know her. I'm sure of that. The New Guys know all about Alexus, don't we? Sure we do."

The old man's smile seemed to dance on his leathery face. It was the smile of a mentally unstable man. He also laughed like a crazy man. In fact, there was no doubt about his state of mind. Steel clanged against steel somewhere behind Jose, loud as a crack of thunder. Jose jumped - as well as he could, bound to a chair - but the man standing by the cow didn't glance up at the sound. It was as though he hadn't heard. His lower lip was thrust out.

"So, you turned on the queen. Not smart. Not a good move. Not a great step for mankind." He flicked his eyes at whoever was standing behind Jose and gave a rapid nod. "Shit happens to guys like you." He let out two more yips, then guided the cow back a little.

The mystery person behind Jose shoved his head forward with one hand and lifted the cow's tail with the other, and he winced in disgust as he realized what they were about to do to him.

His head sank easily into the cow's slimy, shit-caked butt hole. He sucked in a big breath a millisecond before his nose went in and held it. We heard the cow mooing again, and this time he actually *felt* the long moooo. It vibrated throughout his skull. He was neck-deep in a cow's rectum, and it was by far the most disgusting place his head had ever been. He fought down the urge to vomit. His wife was due to have his first daughter in a couple of days, his second child with her. Jose wondered if he would be alive to see it. He didn't think so. Yet this was still hard to believe. Impossible, really.

About thirty seconds later, his head was pulled out of the cow's ass. Face plastered in thick greenish-brown feces; Jose blinked until his eyelashes were un-slimed. Francisco was staring at him with that clownish smile, holding up the smartphone with the glass facing Jose. The nude men with the sharp hooks impaling their backs were alive, and some of them were screaming now, because the hooks were rolling them through the air toward a pair of large spinning saws that were usually used to cut cows like Mr. Shitty Butt in half.

In a better world - a fairer world - he could have lunged for the assault rifle and shot his kidnappers dead, but his hands were bound at the wrists to the chair's heavy steel arms. His torso was bound to the back by more duct tape, thick corsets of the stuff at the waist and just below his sagging man-tits.

His legs were bound to the chair's legs at the knees, the upper calves, the lower calves, and the ankles. And his feet were nailed to the platform. They had been very thorough.

As the saws begun to cut into the flesh and bones of their first victim, Jose turned back to the smartphone Francisco was holding up, and now he realized that, on the phone's screen, there was a woman watching him.

It was Alexus Costilla.

"Well," she said, smiling, "don't you look dapper? How's that new drug empire treating you? I hear you and your pal Julio are making waves in the cartel biz. Why'd you leave Matamoros? Were you not being paid enough?"

Jose just scowled at her. He and the others had abandoned the Matamoros drug cartel - more commonly known as the Costilla Cartel - for damned good reasons, but he wasn't about to give Alexus the pleasure of knowing them.

"Heather, Alexus said, "your boyfriend seems confused. You mind telling him how he got in this shitty situation he's in?"

The sound of heels click-clacking on the steel floor approached from behind him, and Heather appeared from his left. She stood next to Francisco with her hands on the hips of the red Dolce & Gabbana dress he'd gotten her earlier today.

"I talked all your men into taking shots of tequila with me," Heather said. There were tears streaming down her face, but she was smiling like the Castillas. "I laced the tequila with ketamine. Put them right to sleep. Then I needled a smaller dose into you and gave this old guy a call."

"You ungrateful bitch," Jose said through clenched teeth, and a runnel of shit slid off the tip of his nose, oozed down onto his top lip, and crept its way into his mouth. The stench seemed like a living thing, like a brown-green hand crawling down Jose's throat. A fly lit on his nose. He shook his head, and for one second, it went away. It landed on the clump of turd on his right cheek and commenced its lunch.

"I'm not ungrateful, Jose. What I am is grateful for everything Alexus is about to do for me. I'll be on every runway in Paris with her backing. Plus, they're giving me five *million* dollars. Legit money. I'll be everything I've ever wanted to be. I'm sorry, Jose, but I did what I had to do."

"You're so stupid, Heather. Such a dumb blonde cunt," Jose said.

"Kill her," Alexus said.

Heather's eyes got wide, but it was too late. Francisco's hand was already raising a gold-plated revolver to her head. The bullet plowed into the left side of her head an inch or so above the ear. Her brains came out the right side of her head in a spray of blood and fragmented bone, and she went down. The gunshot was deafening. It rang throughout the slaughterhouse.

"Put his head back in there," Alexus said, "and this time leave it."

Jose retched, a deep growling sound. His nose was plugged with wet stink, making it harder for him to draw in a breath to hold this time. His head was shoved back into the cow's rectum. He heard and felt another moo. His bladder let go about forty seconds later, when he realized he was going to suffocate to death with his head stuck in a cow's ass.

King Rio

Chapter 11

"Somebody just whacked Detroit Lenny on Homan, shot him all in the face and chest," Wayne said. "He crashed into Zaniyah's minivan."

"Didn't I say I didn't want no more——"

"It wasn't us, big homie. On cup, we don't know *who* did that shit. Zaniyah just called and told me about it. Her and Lisa was laid up watching a movie when they heard a bunch of gunshots and the crash."

"You mean to tell me," Juice said, standing up, "that Jamal got whacked two nights ago without me giving the order, Styro got killed last night without me giving the order, and now we got another murder in *my* neighborhood without me giving the order? Is that what the fuck I'm hearing?"

"Ain't shit we can do about that, big homie."

"What the fuck do you mean? We *run* this neighborhood."

"It's crackin' out here, big homie. These young niggas out here strapped up, and they ain't hesitating to…"

Wayno was still talking, but Juice tuned him out. Juice had just lost the thread of his thought, because Bubbles was sashaying into the bedroom wearing a skimpy red Mrs. Santa costume that left very little to the imagination, and whatever Wayno was saying no longer mattered.

"What did I tell you about that phone?" she said softly.

"I'll catch you tomorrow, Wayno." Juice ended the call without another word, turned off the phone, and plugged the charger into it, all the while gawking at his stunning girlfriend's jaw-dropping curves.

The minidress barely covered the upper halves of her breasts and the lower halves of her thick buttocks. It was made just like her Santa hat: all red with a thin, furry strip of white at the bottom. Her leather six-inch Chloe heels were also red. She shut and locked the door, hooked her phone up to the Beats Pill speaker on the dresser, and filled the room with the tantalizing Barbadian gibberish of Rihanna.

"Merry Christmas," Bubbles said, and gave his chest a light shove that sent him plopping down onto his side of the bed. She went to the light switch and thumbed it up. His eyes followed her there and back, and she began to bounce and rock her hips from side to side, looking down at him with her lower lip tucked between her teeth.

"Damn," he said hungrily. "Mrs. *Claus*!" He chuckled.

"You like?"

He nodded emphatically, ripping his shirt over his head and tossing it to the floor.

"I figured my dear Santa might deserve a little TLC before he goes flying off in his sleigh to deliver presents to all the good little boys and girls." She lowered the top of her sexy dress and cupped her bare breasts in her hands as she continued to move her hips in the most seductive way.

"Santa is all about this shit right here," Juice said, beaming. He filled his hands with the soft swells of her ass, and the conversations he'd had with Dawn and Wayno a few minutes prior became a distant memory.

She gave him a lap dance, as she had many times in the past at Redbone's Gentleman's club but having her alone in his bedroom was way better. Lakita "Bubbles" Thomas was that special kind of thick, the kind that only black women could naturally possess. She had hips, she had thighs, and God had truly blessed her in the ass department. Juice lay back on the bed with the fingers of his left hand curled around the neck of a big bottle of Hennessey he'd had sitting under the bed-table for a week. He and Bubbles drank down large mouthfuls of the cognac while she danced on his stone-hard, ruler-sized erection.

She eventually shimmied out of the dress. There was nothing but a pair of red-lace thong panties beneath it. Juice pulled a rubber-banded bundle of hundred-dollar bills out of his jeans pocket, snapped the band, and flung the entire stack up toward the whirling white blades of the ceiling fan. $10,000 rained down on the two of them.

"I hope you know I'm keeping all that," she said, turning around to face him. "I would've made that at the club tonight if I was still dancing."

"You gotta work for that," Juice said.

Bubbles climbed onto the bed and stood over his face, making her ass and thighs bounce and shake, her right foot next to his left ear and vice versa. She used her thumbs to push her sexy red thong down to her knees. Juice reached up and tore the thong off with one hard pull.

"You asshole," she griped. "I liked that thong."

"It looks better off than on," he reasoned.

She dropped down, putting her knees where her feet had been, and sat her pussy right on his mouth. "I'll drown your ass," she said, as if it was something he would be afraid of.

In truth, he *loved* it when she sat on his face. He felt that she didn't do it enough - that she *couldn't* do it enough. He stuck out his tongue and licked her ravenously. He held her thighs and dug his tongue deep in between the slick folds of her warm pussy. He sucked on her clitoris and revealed in the mouth-watering aroma of her sex. Moaning softly, she bounced her pussy on his extended tongue. Her tasty juices slid down into his mouth, and he thought it was the most delectable juice he'd ever tasted.

She tried to get up before her orgasm, but he held on and didn't let go. If this meal was costing him ten thousand dollars, then he was going to get the all-you-can-eat special.

He inserted his tongue deep inside of her quivering pussy as she gave herself over to a seismic climax. He could not have been happier to lap up her sweet release. She put her hands on her breasts and loosed a purring moan, slowly gyrating on his hungry mouth.

Spent, she tumbled off to the side of him. He stood up and got rid of his jeans, then grabbed her hips and climbed onto the bed with her, turning her so that the top of her head was on the headboard.

"Santa got some *fire* head," Bubbles said, an amused smile playing around the corners of her mouth. She put her pillow under her head. "Now let me see that south pole." She giggled, moving her fingertips across her taut nipples.

Juice lowered his boxer shorts. The "south pole" popped out, hard and fat and twelve inches long. A drop of precum glistened on its head. He wrapped his fingers around its base and smacked the bulbous head on her exposed clitoris.

Then he penetrated her.

Although it was a tight fit, he slid in easily, the mixture of her orgasmic juices and his saliva acting as a lubricant. He got in about eight or nine inches. It moved into her like an overweight python slithering its way into a waterspout that wasn't quite wide enough to hold it. Her mouth fell agape. She moved her head to the side, and the Mrs. Santa hat went aslant. Out and in, out and in, he pounded his python into her water-spout. She moaned like a porn star: dramatic, high-pitched, and uninhibited. In the background, Rae Sremmurd and Gucci Mane were presenting a compelling theory that they were actually the black version of The Beatles.

She put his pillow over her face to mute the screams, and he took this as unwritten permission to *really* beat the pussy up. He pushed her legs up so that her knees were pinned down by her ears, angling her for deeper penetration, and he began to fuck her hard. Not lovemaking, but merciless, gut-pounding, long-stroking fucking. The type of fucking that would make a younger, less experienced woman tap out. The type of fucking that could *tame* a woman, so to speak.

"You thought it was a game with the south pole, didn't you?" Juice said, smiling at the sound of her muted screams. "It ain't no game with me, baby. This south pole can fuck your whole gravity up. Have your ass on the ceiling. Let me…hear you…talk that shit now."

He was fucking her savagely. The realization that the bullet that had skated over his shoulder this morning could have torn through his neck if it had flown just a few inches to the right crossed his mind, and he fucked Bubbles even harder.

Rae Sremmurd gave way to Future. Wicked, wicked, wicked, wicked, wicked, Juice stood up in the motor and tried to bust the dashboard, only his dashboard was the red maple headboard of his bed. He sped up as he felt the building eruption, and then his dick gushed a hundred million sperm cells into her.

It was his turn to tumble over to the side of her. He took his pillow from off her face, fluffed it a little, and slipped it behind his head. He pulled the covers up over them and kissed Bubbles on the cheek. Her eyes seemed to be focused on the ceiling fan and its four light fixtures. Her chest rose and fell as her breathing stabilized.

"Are you alive over there?" Juice said, chuckling.

"Barely." She smiled. "Shit." She sighed. "Fuck."

"You ain't even gotta give me a Christmas present after that," he said, peeling a hundred-dollar bill off his left elbow.

The afterglow faded, and she turned to face him, resting her left ear on the palm of her left hand and jacking her head up on an elbow. She regarded him with her signature squint of scrutiny. 'I'm telling you now, *Lee*, we're out of this apartment after Christmas is over, because I know that…woman upstairs is here for a reason."

"That's fine with me." At this point, he was willing to agree with Bubbles on just about anything. He had a bunch of thoughts rumbling around in his brain, like these colorful numbered balls in the Illinois Lottery machine. One of them went flying up the chute. "Detroit Lenny just got whacked."

Bubbles gasped. "Really?"

Juice nodded. "And it wasn't even my people who did it."

"Wouldn't it be funny if Shawnna did that, too? That would make her, like, next-level gangster."

"I don't think it would be funny."

"If she got away with it, I mean." Bubbles laughed. "I wouldn't put it past her. She's already been on a knockout spree. Somebody needs to make a movie about her. She's more gangster than most of these niggas around her, and to top it all off, she's four months pregnant. Now I see why Mya calls Shawnna her favorite sister. Your daughter is the truth."

Shaking his head, Juice reached for his iPhone. He didn't pick it up, but he did turn it on, just in case Shawnna *had* committed the murder and was trying to reach him. Another colorful ball of thought came rocketing up the chute.

"Dawn asked me if I think Alexus is involved with a Mexican drug cartel," he said, lacing his fingers together on top of his head.

"Oh, she is," Bubbles said without a moment's hesitation. "And to tell you the truth, her influence on the drug market in this country is unbelievable. I learned a lot about her operation when I was with Blake. She has everybody in her pocket. All the Republicans, all the Democrats; all the judges, top police officials, bankers, and the news media. If you remember, when Alexus and her family got indicted, the media was calling their drug organization the Costilla Cartel. The charges were dropped, the main snitch - her uncle Flako - was found floating in the Rio Grande, and no news network has ever mentioned the Costilla Cartel since then. It might sound crazy to say this, but I think Alexus is probably more powerful than any drug cartel boss in history. She might even be more powerful than the president. And I know they have her on record as having only a billion dollars more than Bill Gates, but I'm willing to bet she has at least double that. At *least*."

"Yeah, and you're the real Mrs. Claus," Juice said sarcastically.

"You don't have to believe me."

"Good."

"It's the truth, though."

"Sure it is," Juice said doubtfully. "Get up and turn off that light."

She sucked her teeth as she threw back the covers. Her eyes never left his as she got out of bed and crossed the room to the light switch, and his never left her big round ass. God, she was stunning. Bubbles was one of those women who actually looked better naked than she did with clothes on. Long black hair, pretty brown eyes, and creamy caramel skin all the way down to her frosted red toenails.

"You have the most incredible body I've ever seen," he said.

"You're just saying that now. As soon as Porsha Williams or Val Warner comes on TV, you'll be staring at them."

"No, I mean it. Really."

"Well, thank you," she said, blushing as she returned to bed. "I've been working on it a lot lately. It's easy to stay in shape working the pole every night, but since I haven't been at the club ever since the day we got together, it's been getting harder. We need to start working out together."

"We just did."

"You know what I mean." Smiling with the left side of her face sunken into her pillow, she put her hand on his belly and gave it a rub. "Either we start working out together or I'm going back to Redbone's. The choice is yours."

He shook his head. "You strip for me now." He paused, thinking. "I know how people always talk about men not liking the fact that their girl's a stripper after they *met* her at the strip club, but I'm different. I actually wanted you before I even met you. I wanted you when I was in prison watching them talk about you and Bulletface on BET news and TMZ. Then it was you and Young Meach, which I personally thought was kind of fucked up since Meach is signed to Money Bagz Management. That's like going from Birdman to Wayne, or from Rick Ross to Meek Mill."

"I did that shit on purpose," Bubbles explained. "I'm not a hoe, but he was playing me, so I played his ass right back. Blake had me and this ratchet ass girl named Janautica living with him at a mansion he had in Miami. I hated that girl so bad. She used to say the stupidest shit. 'I just went out yonder, ya feel me like … I just got these gold *skreeks* in my hair to match my watch, ya feel me like I don't know what he saw in that skinny bitch, but he used to be kissing all on her, right in front of me. So, I bought some condoms one night and fucked him, Young D, *and* Meach right in the same room with him. Of course, I wouldn't do that now. I was young and insecure back then."

"Where was Alexus?"

"She was with T-Walk, I think. She had left Blake for T-Walk, then she was back with Blake again, then back with T-

Walk. She used them, really. That's how I see it. They thought they were using her for money, but I think she was using them for sex. I wouldn't be surprised if she starts fucking T-Walk, now that he's back."

"Dawn just said that too," he said.

"Oh yes. It's very possible. T-Walk showed up at her restaurant when she took me and the girls out for dinner last night. She hugged him and everything. I should have snapped a picture of *that*, since she made such a big deal about Blake's picture with me."

Juice's cell phone vibrated on the bed-table. He reached for it and saw that it was a picture message from Shawnna. He opened it. It was a screenshot of an Instagram post from The Shade Room, a photo of Alexus gugging T-Walk beside a table. Bubbles, Tamera, Tirzah and Alexus's lawyer, Nikkia Staples, were all seated around the table with half-empty plates of seafood placed in front of them. The photo was captioned: *Merry Christmas, TSR Roommates! Looks like some of you were right! Wonder if Bulletface is gonna bust his gun at her this time! #BaeWatch #TWalksBack!!*

Juice handed the phone to Bubbles and let her see it with her own eyes.

"Looks like somebody beat you to the punch," he said.

King Rio

Chapter 12

It was two o'clock a.m. Pacific Time, and the calm in Rita-Mae Bishop's fifty-million-dollar Calabasas mansion was almost preternatural. This was especially surprising considering that it was Christmas morning and there were four young children anxious to wake up and tear into their presents.

Rita had been in the holiday spirit all week long. She had a vast collection of "ugly Christmas" sweaters and three whole gallons of homemade eggnog, and she'd spent tens of thousands of dollars on exterior decorations, making her place the jolliest mansion in all of Calabasas, California.

Now it was Christmas Day - just barely, but still - Rita was standing in her marble-floored foyer, gazing up at the lighted star at the top of her 25-foot tree (which was encircled at the trunk by gift-wrapped boxes stacked ten feet high) and sipping gingerly from a crystal glass of brandy-laced nog. Her daughter, Alexus, had awakened her for a talk. Alexus was next to her, sipping an expensive Italian vodka from a solid gold champagne glass. Rita had on an ugly Christmas sweater, and she had tried talking Alexus into wearing one. But to Alexus, if it wasn't all-white, it wasn't all right. Alexus donned a white Atelier Versace dress and white Jimmy Choo pumps.

"You're becoming too much of a diva," Rita said, a small smile threatening to upturn the corner of her mouth.

"You're one to talk," Alexus said, and she also had a burgeoning smile. "I saw your show Wednesday. You practically climbed in Denzel's lap."

"I did not."

"Mm-hmm."

The Rita Bishop Show was the most-watched daytime talk show on television. Now on its third season, the show was

Rita's pride and joy. She was known for openly flirting with the actors she found attractive, and anyone who watched the show knew that Denzel Washington was her absolute number-one crush. But Alexus didn't need to watch the show to know that her mom had been head-over-hills for Denzel for as far back as she could remember.

"I couldn't go too hard on him," Rita said. "His wife was in the audience. I told her she was the luckiest woman in the universe. But the good lord knows... *mmm*... if that man was *single*."

"You are so disgusting."

"I would've gotten more than dis——"

"Uuugh! Stop, Ma. You're ruining my taste for Denzel movies." Alexus snickered. "Old people are so nasty nowadays. Bunch of sickos. I remember seeing somewhere that nursing homes have some of the highest rates of STDs. Now I'm starting to see why."

Rita gave her an icy look. "I am forty-eight years *young*, thank you very much." She drank from her glass. "What do you want to talk about?"

"I did something stupid," Alexus said. "Twice, actually."

"Tell me something I don't know."

"I, uh...I cheated," Alexus whispered.

"Already? T-Walk works fast," Rita whispered back.

"No, not with T-Walk. It was with somebody named Sincere. They call him Rell. He's from Chicago. One of the boys Blake was hanging out with last night. It was three of us. Rell's girlfriend - no, they're married, I think. Yeah, so...it was me, Rell, and his wife. Her name's Tamera. We had a threesome in an empty dressing room at the Deja and D-Boy concert last night."

"And you got the nerve to call *me* nasty?"

"I know. I was drunk, and I was still kind of mad about Blake taking that pic with the girl he was cheating on me with last year. I guess I wanted some payback." She shrugged dismissively. "What goes around comes around. And that boy was fine as hell."

"You are wrong on so many levels, Alexus. So, so many. You're right about Blake cheating on you, but two wrongs don't make a right. You just got bailed out of jail for shooting a freaking gun at Blake for taking a picture with——"

"I know, Ma."

"It's ridiculous, Alexus."

"I told you I did something stupid."

"You said twice."

"Yeah, I also…umm I'll just show you." Alexus raised her iPhone and went to Instagram. Her page popped up first, and Rita scoffed at how many followers she had.

"A hundred and twenty million people," Rita said. "Are you still number-one on there?"

Alexus nodded. "Then it's Selena Gomez with a hundred and three million."

"Mary J. Blige *should* be the most followed person on there."

With a brief chuckle, Alexus thumbed her way to The Shade Room page and showed her mom the photo. Rita brought a hand up to her chest (effectively covering Rudolph's very shiny nose on that ugly sweater she was wearing), sucked in a gasp, and turned to Alexus. Her eyes shifted from Alexus to the photo and back to Alexus again.

"Has Blake seen this?" Rita asked, after a time.

"No. It just got posted a few hours ago. He's been asleep since it was posted."

"When was this picture taken?"

"Last night, when I took those girls to dinner at my restaurant."

"Give them some money to take it down. Have Britney or Nikkia contact——"

"That won't work. This pic has been screenshotted and reposted probably a million times already. There's nothing I could possibly do to get this picture erased. It'll be on every gossip site there is within the next four or five hours. Not that I care what anybody else thinks. It's Blake I'm worried about. You know how quick he'll cut all ties with me if he so much as *thinks* I did anything with T-Walk."

"Well, did you?"

"No," Alexus said, a little louder than intended. She lowered her voice back to a whisper. "It was only a hug. He asked me for a hug, I gave him a hug, and he left. That's all it was."

"That's not how Blake's gonna look at it."

"I know," Alexus said defeatedly. Tears gathered along her lower eyelids. "I don't know what to do. I don't want to lose my husband, Mama. You know how good it's been between me and him ever since Juan was born. When he sees this picture, he is going to flip. Especially since I just flipped out on him for the pic he took with Bubbles. It makes it seem like I was intentionally making a fool of him, like I did it on purpose. As soon as he wakes up and checks his phone, he's gonna lose it."

Rita became thoughtful. She finished off what was left in her glass. "Well," she said finally, "I believe the answer is right there in your problem."

"What's that supposed to mean?"

"If he's gonna lose it as soon as he wakes up and checks his phone, then you need to make sure he doesn't see his phone when he wakes up."

"And how am I supposed to do that?" Alexus said as the tears went streaking down her cheeks. "He checks his phone every morning just like the rest of us. How am I supposed to stop him from doing that?"

"You'll figure it out," Rita said, yawning. "If your marriage is as important to you as you say it is, you'll find a way to get through this. If all else fails, call on Jesus." She headed toward the elevator at the rear of the foyer, which wasn't really necessary since it only took a good minute to get to the second floor using the stairs. "I'm going back to bed until those little angels wake me back up in an hour or less. I'd suggest you get started on a plan to save your marriage... and this Christmas."

Alexus sighed, thumb-knuckled the tears from her face, and swallowed down the rest of her vodka. It played like a blowtorch in her throat; it strengthened her resolve. She paced a tight circle in front of the towering tree, thinking, thinking, thinking, biting the inside of her cheek. Then she came up with a plan to keep her husband from going ballistic on this beautiful Christmas Day.

King Rio

Chapter 13

Blake liked it when his wife was spontaneous like this.

He had just woke up to the sound and feel of her fellating him, sucking his erection in and out of her throat. He scraped the nail of a forefinger at the corners of his eyes, ridding them of the crust, and blinked a couple of times.

The bedroom was enormous, and not because it was made this way. Alexus had had two bedrooms combined into one. The walls and the floor were white Carrera marble, and everything else was 24-karat gold. The bedposts, the tables, the two fireplaces, the lamps, the chandeliers, and the dressers - all so shiny and gold you'd think Trinidad James had furnished the place. Even the curtains were made of gold.

Breakfast was waiting on a gold cart next to their California King bed: a T-bone steak, cheese eggs, grape jelly spread over toasted raisin bread, and a tall glass of cold orange juice. The biggie breakfast is what he was fond of calling it, and Alexus knew it was his favorite combo of foods to eat in the morning.

A grin stretched across the bottom of his handsome dark face. He looked down at Alexus and chuckled once. She was naked, in a position that was close to a sixty-nine, her ass tooted up in the air to the right of him, her head slightly angled to the right to give her the straight on sixty-nine position she needed to successfully take him to the back of her throat with every drop of her head.

He smacked a hand onto her big round ass and shook it. "Well," he said, watching the beads of saliva bubbling out from the corners of her mouth and rolling down the sides of his long black phallus, "Merry Christmas to you, too."

He picked up his gold plate of breakfast and a gold fork from the cart and shoveled a forkful of eggs in his mouth. He'd fallen asleep with a Hublot watch heavily drizzled in white VVS diamonds clasped around his left wrist, and now he looked at it. Just as he noted the time - it was 3:51 Pacific Time - he heard the rapid thump of footsteps beyond the bedroom's gold door.

"It's Christmas, it's Christmas, it's Christmas!" Blake's two five-year-olds shouted in unison. They were King Neal, Blake and Alexus's son, and Blake King Jr., alias Bee Bee, whose mother was Tiffany Jenkins, a woman Blake had only slept with once. As the saying goes, that's all it took. He'd found out about Bee Bee last year, and he'd been keeping the boy every weekend since.

"Daddy, can we open out gifts now?" It was Savaria, also known as Vari, his nine-year-old daughter. "Grandma said we gotta ask you first."

"Yeah, go ahead."

"Okay, Merry Christmas!"

"Merry Christ-mas," he said, forcing the word out in two syllables separated by a gasp for air as Alexus took his dick all the way down her throat and held it there.

Blake was not a minute-man. In fact, it usually took him quite a while to ejaculate. But Alexus had a way with her mouth that never failed to push him over the edge within minutes. At 3:55 a.m., his dick tapped out. Alexus sucked on the twitching, spurting head until she'd emptied it of every drop. She spit it onto the head and sucked it off several times as his hard muscle softened in her hands, and then she swallowed.

"Merry Christmas, Blakey," she said, planting soft kisses on his sharply defined abdomen. He had the six-pack of a pro bodybuilder, and she loved kissing on each individual muscle. She tucked his flaccid penis back into his silk Versace boxer shorts.

"You're a dirty, nasty-mouthed mu'fucka," Blake said, his face twisted with disgust and the hint of a smirk.

She lay down next to him, smiling. "Can I get a good morning kiss?"

"You can get a good morning kick." He began to eat. The steak was well-seasoned and tender, just the way he liked it.

Alexus got up and put on a curve-hugging white dress and matching heels. Her hair was long and as straight as a length of thread, and she'd dyed it blonde. Her wrists, neck and ears were blinging with hundreds of carats of flawless white diamonds.

Chewing a piece of steak, Blake said, "I think I'm about done kissing you. From now on, it's hugs only. Fuck that kissing. You got a white girl's mouth."

She laughed. "Whatever," she said, rolling her eyes, shaking her head, and smiling, all at the same time.

"I'm serious as a heart attack," Blake said. "Every time you suck my dick, you swallow. That's some nasty shit."

"No, it's actually not." She stood beside the bed with her hands on her hips.

"Uh, yes, it actually is," he said.

"You're my husband. I'm supposed to do shit like that."

"How many other men have you fucked with in the past that have gotten that same treatment?"

Her smile widened. "None."

"You're the biggest liar I've ever met in my life."

"I'm not lying. I've never swallowed anybody else's... stuff. Ugh, can we please not talk about this?" she said with another shake of the head. "Let's discuss good things. Like the fact that the guy who's been threatening to murder you wife is no longer a threat."

"That's what you should be ugh'ing about." Blake had been standing next to her chair when her coked-up uncle's goons had forced Jose's head into the cow's asshole. "That was some sick shit."

"Would you rather kiss him after that or kiss me after I suck your dick?"

"I'd rather shoot him and slap you."

"Keep that up and you'll be the next one with your head up a cow's ass."

"What's up with his partner, though?"

She shrugged. "We're looking. He was last seen in Mexico City. I'm hoping we can catch him sooner than later. Enrique thinks he's the more dangerous of the Padilla-Chavez Cartel's top two bosses. Jose was just a big talker. He was always too high to do any real thinking. Enrique believes it's the other one - Julio - who's the real threat. He's the mastermind. It was Julio who brought the idea of leaving my family's business to Jose and the others, and if the information we've been given is accurate, it was also Julio Chaves who put the million-dollar bounty on my head."

"He won't get past Enrique."

"Hopefully not," Alexus said, curling her fingers to regard her fingernails. "So, do you think that new Chicago guy will be able to step into Cup's shoes? He looked like the hustling type. What was his name again? Juice?"

"Yeah." Blake set his empty plate down on the food cart, picked up the glass of orange juice, and took a drink as he glanced to his bedside table for his iPhone.

It wasn't there.

His two heavy white diamond necklaces were there. His four packets of bank-new-hundred-dollar bills were there. His five-million-dollar-encrusted pinkie ring was there. His last two sticks of Big Red chewing gum were there. But his iPhone 7 plus was missing in action.

"Where the fuck is my phone?" he said, and immediately turned to Alexus. She was still looking at her fingernails, but that sneaky little smile had returned.

"No phones today," she said. "Let's make today a family day. It's Christmas. We need to be having fun with the kids."

Blake stared at her blankly for a moment. "You're lucky you woke me up the right way," he said finally.

"Of course, I did. Hubby."

Her expression became triumphant as he got out of bed. She followed him into their bathroom, which had his and hers sinks and toilets, a large claw foot bathtub, and an eight-person glass-doored shower. Everything was gold.

He washed his face and started brushing his diamond-encrusted platinum teeth, while Alexus kissed on the back of his shoulders and fondled his chest and abs with her wandering fingernails.

"If Juice can move that shipment as fast as Cup used to," she said, "we might be able to take over Chicago again. Remember how Cup had that whole city on lock? I think he might have sold more bricks than any other black guy we've done business with. All those so-called trap niggas on your record label got lazy once they got a few million in the bank. If Biggs got back in the game, I bet he'd be able to take over whatever parts of Chicago that Juice can't reach. I know our boy Fly is doing his thing or whatever, but his ass is getting lazy too. My people go through way too much getting that product into this country to be slow-grinding the shit off."

Her frustration was understandable. For years - maybe even decades - the Costilla Cartel had pumped hundreds of tons of cocaine, heroin, and marijuana into the United States through a drug tunnel that ran from beneath their family-owned restaurant in Matamoros, Mexico to the basement of a house in Brownsville, Texas. But unfortunately the drug tunnel had been discovered earlier this year by some Mexican journalist with a death wish (his wish was granted weeks later when he was gunned down at a Matamoros traffic light), and now the Costilla Cartel had to work harder to get their product into the States.

They moved their drugs via private airplanes, submarines, container ships, fishing vessels, buses, tractor-trailers, and cars. The drugs were held in safe houses in southern California before being shipped to Chicago and elsewhere. The 1,000 kilograms of cocaine that had been delivered to Chicago for Juice had actually arrived on an Amtrak train at Union Station.

Blake spit out a mouthful of bubbly white Colgate Total foam. "Be patient, baby. Goddamn. I'm sorry if I don't want the Feds investigating my artists right now. MBM is a record label. A *successful* record label. I want it to stay that way. I want my artists to focus on making good music. We'll leave the hustling to the trap niggas that ain't got no other way to get it. Let's just sit back and see what Juice can do. Shit, he ain't even been back in Chicago a full day yet. Give him a few weeks. We'll see how shit works out. If it ain't good for us, we'll cut him loose. Give him some time to make some moves. You gotta remember where he's at. I wouldn't be surprised if they got shot at soon as they made it home."

He went back to brushing his teeth. In the gold-framed mirror's reflection, he observed his wife's sexy face peak from around his right shoulder. She hugged him tightly with her cheek pressed against his shoulder, and he briefly considered striking her forehead with his toothbrush.

"I love you so much, Blake," she said softly. "Your last name fits you so perfectly, because you are truly my King."

Blake spit. "Oh, *now* I'm your king. The other day you tried to do me like *Martin Luther* King got done at the Lorraine Hotel, but now I'm your king."

"He'd still be alive if he hadn't been at that hotel cheating on his wife. Ha! You fell right into that one."

"Don't lie on my nigga Martin like that."

"I'm not lying. Check the facts. The lady he was cheating with ended up being a Kentucky senator. That wondering penis must run in the King bloodline."

Blake chuckled, gargling a cap full of mouthwash. This was news to him; he'd never heard of Mr. I Had A Dream also being known as Mr. I Had A Side Chick. He spit out the mouthwash and splashed some water around in the sink to get rid of the toothpaste spatter.

"You need to be over there brushing your teeth," he said, turning around to face Alexus.

She poised her lips for a kiss and tried to peck on onto his mouth, but he palmed her pretty face and shoved it aside.

"Don't get beat up on Christmas," he threatened, and reached down to fill his hands with her big butt.

"What kinda husband doesn't kiss his wife?"

"The kind a husband who wakes up one day and realizes his wife is a thot."

"I'm not a——"

"Slurp."

"Asshole."

"Slurp."

"I asked you to stop saying that to me."

"Sluuuurp," he said, stretching the word.

She clamped her hands around the front of his neck. "Say it again, you black ass bastard. I'll choke you to death."

He laughed, grabbed her wrists, and slammed them down to her sides. Her sexy green eyes gazed into his deep brown ones. He felt his dick begin to swell in his boxers, but he wasn't about to give it to her. She wasn't getting the dick until he got the iPhone.

He stepped around her, and she jumped onto his back as he returned to their bedroom. He fell back on the bed to detach the piggyback rider, then pulled on the red designer jeans and Timbs he'd set on the arm of the sofa at the foot of the bed after he'd bathed last night. He was sliding his arms into the sleeves of a matching shirt when Alexus said something that made him turn and look at her to see whether or not she was kidding him.

"I'm gonna let you have a threesome before the New Year. Any girl you wanna pick." She was on her feet again, walking to him. "So, who's it gonna be?"

He finished putting the shirt on and stood up. She was right in front of him, hands on her generous hips, perfume drifting up into his nostrils and making him weak with desire.

"A threesome?" he said, as if he hadn't heard her right the first time.

She nodded. "That's what I said. And you can pick the girl."

"What's the catch?"

"Pick a girl first."

"I can't just pick a girl. She might be in a faithful relationship with——"

"Oh please. Don't kid yourself. Every bitch in the industry wants to fuck you just like every nigga wants to fuck me."

"Every nigga wants to fuck *you*? He shook his head, gritting his teeth. "No. They want Ing Die."

"Every nigga wants to fuck Ing Die?" She paused, thinking, then burst out laughing. "Oh. Fucking Die." She loosed another laugh. "You're so dumb."

"If the catch is you fucking some other guy," he said, "you got me all the way fucked up. I'm telling you that now."

She rolled her eyes, shook her head, and exhaled loudly as he grabbed his things from his bedside table. He put his jewelry on and pocketed the cash, and they left out of the bedroom together.

"The catch is," Alexus said, "you and I are in the Stone Age for the rest of the day. No phone calls, no Internet, no social media. Just me, you, my mom, and the kids."

Piece of cake, Blake thought, rubbing his hands together as he thought of all the possibilities. Who would he invite into the bedroom for a threesome with him and his beautiful wife? Would it be one of his old side chicks? He knew Bubbles wasn't an option, but maybe Tasia "Baddie Barbie" Olsen was willing to participate. He had thousands of sexy black women who would not hesitate to join him and Alexus in bed, and if all he had to do was not get on a phone or on the Internet today, then he was going to do just that.

King Rio

Chapter 14

"Ooh, girl, Bulletface is going to go nuts when he sees that pic of T-Walk and Alexus all hugged up together. You know he's seen it by now," Shawnna said.

"So you expect me to just sit here and act like you didn't kick my ass last night?" Dawn replied sleepily.

Shawnna smiled. She was sitting up in bed in the master bedroom at the Villa Taj, Bankroll Reese's big white mansion in Burr Ridge. Reese was asleep next to her. She had decided against going with him to The Visionary Lounge last night. Instead, she had stayed here in bed and watched *Pretty Woman* with Richard Gere and Julia Roberts. She'd dreamt about Reese taking *her* shopping on Rodeo Drive, and when he came to bed about an hour ago - it was 6:10 Central Time now - she had smiled like she was smiling now, keeping her eyes shut as he eased beneath the covers with her. He'd kissed her on the cheek, and she had smelled weed on his breath. Seconds later he'd fallen into a deep, unmoving sleep.

She had only been awake five minutes or so, long enough to empty her bladder, brush her teeth, remove her headscarf, rinse her face, return to bed and call her sister, whose ass she'd kicked last night.

"You don't look like I kicked your ass." She was on a Facetime video call with Dawn. "I apologize, sister. I know I was in the wrong. I was just so mad at you for doing that stupid ass shit."

"I know. I apologize too."

"Where's Mama?"

"She slept in my bed. Not sure if she's up yet."

"Is she still mad at me?"

"Mad is an understatement," Dawn said. "She's ready to kill somebody.'

With a short, quick giggle, Shawnna unfolded her legs and stepped down off the bed. She crossed the thick black wall-to-wall carpet barefoot and stood at the large picture window. She'd left the bed because she didn't want to disturb Reese's sleep, and for the same reason she pulled the shut curtain back a couple of inches instead of opening it all the way.

The window overlooked the long, winding driveway that stretched from the wrought-iron gate at the front of the property to the large rectangle of blacktop in front of the mansion. The grounds were layered in snow and there were still more flakes of God's cold dandruff sprinkling down from the sky above.

"It's not funny," Dawn said. "You punched out Mother."

"I don't think it's funny. Not that I punched her. That was honestly an accident. I was just thinking about all the times she whooped our asses with belts and switches and extension cords when daddy went to prison. That mean-ass left hook was probably just some part of my brain remembering that shit."

"She's going to kill you."

"The sooner I die," Shawnna said, "The sooner I get to see our brother again. I stopped being scared to die at his funeral."

"Did you confront Reese about him and Myesha?"

"Kinda sorta. Something went down right when I was getting to it."

"Did it have anything to do with Detroit Lenny?"

Shawnna put on a look of mock surprise. "What about Detroit Lenny?"

"He got killed on Homan. Somebody shot him up in his truck."

"Damn, for real?"

Dawn squinted and said nothing.

"What?" Shawnna said, wearing the guiltiest smirk she could muster.

"Don't let me find out you had something to do with that, Shawnna. Fighting is one thing, but that - that's serious. You could lose your life. Either to prison or to somebody else's gun."

"No need to preach that sermon to me. I'm not a gangbanger. You know I use hands, not guns."

"Bullshit. You just blew a hole in Big Wanda's shoulder a couple months ago."

"Yeah," Shawnna said, turning to look at Reese's sleeping figure, "but I only did that to save your ass. They shouldn't have tried to jump you. But I'm not crazy. I wouldn't kill somebody. Not even Big Yachty."

Dawn laughed and shook her head. "Well, back to what you said about Bulletface, I don't know if he's seen that picture or not, but I know he'll see it sometime today. It was all over Facebook before I went to bed. I'm about to go downstairs and ask Bubbles about it. You know he actually has his cell phone number."

"I wish I had the phone number to a nigga worth almost two billion dollars. None of my exes are even worth two *thousand* dollars."

"I would've definitely poked a hole in *that* condom," Dawn said, and chuckled twice. "That ass-whooping would be worth it."

"Oh, I wouldn't need you to do that. As fine as Bulletface is, I would've rode that thang until I got pregnant and went into labor."

"Shawnna, you already got a fine-ass nigga."

"Yeah, but he ain't two-billion-dollar fine."

"Then it's your job to build him up to that level. He's *sixty*-million-dollar fine, and that's better than most rappers - big-time rappers. Take control before another bitch takes your place. So what if he cheats? You know which head most men think with that one, you need to be thinking for the other one. Help him turn that sixty million into six *hundred* million, and while you're at it get him to lend you the money to get us another hair salon. We should have a second salon before you pop that baby out."

Shawnna bit her thumbnail lightly between her teeth. "You're right," she said.

"I'm always right," Dawn said.

"Tell Ra'Mya I said Merry Christmas."

"I love that kid. She's so innocent."

"She's our new little sister," Shawnna said pridefully.

"Don't corrupt her."

Shawnna rolled her eyes. "Bye, bitch. I'll be there around noon."

"Merry Christmas, Grinch."

"Merry Christmas, skank."

Call ended, Shawnna lowered the phone to her side, plucked out her earbuds, and gazed thoughtfully at Reese. She wondered if he'd fucked another bitch at his nightclub last night, got mad about it, and went into the connected bathroom to get him out of her sight.

Although she had taken a long bath before going to bed, she filled the tub with soap and burning-hot water, added a bit of cold water to make it bearable, and sat in the bathtub for a full twenty minutes, listening to The Weeknd's album through her earbuds and trying not to think about all the nasty places Reese's dick had been.

It didn't work.

Images of Reese fucking Myesha flashed before her mind's eye. She was suddenly proud of herself for making him wear protection from the very beginning. She pictured tiny little monsters that were sexually transmitted diseases and infections, Furby-looking purple creatures with razor-sharp spikes on their backs and a million equally sharp teeth in their mouths, riding on Reeses's sperm the way cowboys rode on the backs of horses. "Gonna munch on this bitch's red blood cells," the purple monster in the lead said, inciting histrionics and screams of agreement from the others.

Shawnna had a vivid imagination.

She got out of the tub, drained the water, lotioned, deodorized, and perfumed, and then padded naked to Reese's walk-in closet, regarding him distastefully as she passed the bed.

He'd taken her on several shopping sprees over the past few months, and half of the clothes and shoes were here in his closet. She selected fitted black yoga pants and a hot-pink curve-hugging V-neck T-shirt. Her baby bump was hardly visible, her ever-growing breasts were now D-cups, and her ass was still fat and round and incredibly soft. She put on a pair of Nike Air Max sneakers, looked at herself in the mirror, muttered a self-approving "yaaass," and walked back out to the bedroom.

She picked up her purse, dropped her phone in it, and lifted her gun out of it. She detached the extended magazine, asked herself how many rounds she'd pumped into Detroit Lenny's white Ford Explorer, and then laughed as she reattached the clip. *Guess old Detroit Lenny wasn't built Ford tough*, she thought to herself.

She went around to Reese's side of the bed and picked up his gun. Like hers, it too had a 30-round clip. She wondered if there was a round in the chamber of his gun as she peeled the sheet and blanket down to his ankles and straddled him.

One way to find out seemed better than the other way.

She pointed the gun at his pillow, a couple of inches away from his right ear, and squeezed the trigger.

The gun fired, and a hole appeared in the pillow.

His eyes popped open to find the barrels of two pistols trained on his face.

"What the fuck is wrong with you?" he said in a sleepless stupor.

"*You're* what's wrong with me," she said, gritting her teeth. "You think I'm a dumb bitch. You think I'm gonna just lay down whenever your little diseased dick gets hard so you can pump me full of purple monsters. But guess what? I ain't going for it."

"Purple monsters? What the hell are you talking about?"

"Oh, you know. Don't play dumb now." She climbed off him and kneeled on her side of the bed, keeping her gun aimed at his face but swinging his over to aim at his crotch. "I'll blow your goddamn dick off."

"Shawnna——"

"Shut the fuck up."

"Baby——"

"*Shut...the fuck...up.*" She jammed the barrel of her gun into his cheek. "I'm not playing with you, Reese. Speak when I ask you to speak or lose your dick. You understand that?"

He nodded his head. "Yeah," he said carefully.

"Now," Shawnna said, "you dirty-dick bitch, you fucked my best friend and got her pregnant. Fucked her *raw*. And you *know* she was my best friend. Who does that? Oh, wait - I know who does that. *Tyrece* does that. Bankroll fucking Reese does that. Bankroll fucking Reese fucks his girlfriend's best friend like it's cool thing to do."

She began to rock back and forth a little. She suddenly realized tears were rolling down her face. She had a vision:

Reese sliding his dick into Myesha's polluted pussy and holding it there while the tiny purple monsters - born and bred inside that frequently used cave of a pussy - packed their bags, waved goodbye to their monster parents, and moved into Reese's balls. She laughed at the image and shook her head as someone approached the door.

"Y'all good in there?" It was Chubb, Reese's overweight bodyguard.

"Get the fuck away from me, Chubb. I already shot one fat nigga. Don't fuck around and be the second one, okay? Leave us alone," Shawnna said.

"Reese?" Chubb shouted, and the doorknob shook.

Shawnna raised the gun from Reese's crotch to the door.

"I'm good, big homie," Reese said.

"You sure? Shay said she heard a gunshot."

"I'm *good*," Reese insisted. "Tell Shay to roll me a blunt."

"Yup. I'll be right back." There were heavy foot-falls beyond the door that quickly faded to nothing.

Shawnna moved backward on her knees, lowered her feet to the floor, and slowly lowered the guns down to her sides. She began to pace from one end of the room to the other, tears blurring her sight and dripping off her chin. She knew what she was doing was wrong. She knew there had to be a more healthy way to go about resolving this domestic dispute. She just couldn't think clearly right now. She wanted to shoot Reese *and* Myesha.

"Are you fucking your assistant too?" She was walking toward the bed again, blinking away the tears. "Are you and Shay mixing monsters? Huh? Tell me the truth."

"Shay is only my assistant, baby."

"Swear to God."

"I swear on my father's grave me and Shay have never done anything sexual. Why would I do that when I know how close she is with Bubbles?"

"Oh," Shawnna said, stopping at the foot of the bed, "so you won't fuck my daddy's *girlfriend's* best friend, but you'll fuck *my* best friend. I see."

"Baby, it ain't even like that."

"Yeah, it is like that," Shawnna said, raising the guns again. "It's *just* like that."

She aimed and opened fire.

Chapter 15

"Merry Christmas, Daddy," Dawn said, giving Juice a hug and a peck on the cheek as he opened the door for her to enter his first-floor apartment.

She followed him into the living room and found Ra'Mya kneeling beside the Christmas tree, tearing open a gift-wrapped box that turned out to be a brand-new iPhone 7 plus. Bubbles and her cousin Tamia were on the sofa with Wayno, whose right arm was in a sling.

"Merry Christmas, everybody!" Dawn shrieked.

"Merry Christmas!" everybody replied.

"Mya, Shawnna told me to tell you she said Merry Christmas."

"I'll text her again," Ra'Mya said. "I sent her a Merry Christmas text a few minutes ago. She hasn't even read it yet."

Dawn was itching to open her presents, but she didn't want to risk looking like a kid in front of Wayno's fine ass. Plus, she had some exclusive Queen A questions for Bubbles. She stood next to the arm of the sofa, smiling not because she was in the Christmas spirit, but because she'd caught Wayno's eyes on the ass of her jeans as she walked past him. Knowing that he was here, she had purposely worn her tightest pair of jeans with Gucci belt and six-inch Christian Louboutin boots that made her already melonesque derriere stick out even further. A dash of Chanel perfume across the neckline of her gray sequined Ralph Lauren sweater guaranteed to hold him spellbound. He'd told her just last week how irresistible he found the perfume to be when Tamia had borrowed some from Bubbles, so she'd gone out and bought herself a few bottles of it.

"Bubbles," she said, "you *have* to tell me about Alexus."

"She's crazy. There, you happy?" Bubbles said.

"She's not crazy." Dawn laughed. "What did she say? What did she eat? And what the heck was T-Walk doing there?"

"The only reason she invited us out to dinner was for damage control. She had just bonded out of jail for shooting a gun at her husband for taking a picture with us - well, for taking a picture with *me*, because that's what she was *really* mad about - and she wanted to tie all the loose strings. Her lawyer showed up at our hotel, like, thirty minutes before Alexus was released from the county jail. We picked her up, she had a glam team get her hair and makeup together, and then we went and had dinner at her restaurant."

"Which is when T-Walk came into the picture."

Bubbles nodded. "She was actually sitting there crying when all of a sudden he walked up and touched her shoulder. I don't know where he came from. He just kinda popped outta nowhere. They didn't do much talking. Just a couple of words and a quick hug, then he was gone and we were on our way to the concert. Her lawyer had us sign non-disclosure agreements, basically saying we can't discuss the shooting or anything else about Blake and Alexus with the media. The lawyer cut fifty-thousand-dollar checks to all three of us. Then we got drunk and did grown-up things."

"Grown-up thing?" Dawn said.

"For real," Tamia said. "What's that supposed to mean?"

Bubbles smiled and glanced over at her younger cousin. "Let's just say you and Alexus grew from the same tree."

It was no secret that Tamia Thomas was one of the most promiscuous girls in North Lawndale. Dawn didn't have enough fingers and toes to count all the dicks Tamia had sucked, and those were just the ones she knew she knew about. Which made it all the more mind boggling that Wayno was actually dating the loose young thot. Sure, Tamia was a bad bitch - short and cute-faced with an enormous butt. She was practically a shorter version of Bubbles. But she was still a thot.

"What do you mean by that?" Dawn asked, curious to know if Bubbles was implying that Alexus was cheating on Blake.

Bubbles ran two fingers across her lips, zipping them shut.

"Don't ask; don't tell," she said. "Oi fully intends to abide by the rules of that non-disclosure agreement. Her business is hers and mine is mine. I just wanted that check."

Tamia asked Bubbles to loan her $2,500, and while Bubbles offered an endless list of reasons why she would do no such thing, Dawn stared at Wayno, who had joined Juice at the dining room table. The two men were seated and leaning toward each other, speaking in low tones. Wayno was putting on his red leather Pelle Pelle jacket. Like Juice, he wore a hooded sweater over jeans and wheat Timbs. His long dreadlocks were pulled back in a ponytail, revealing that ridiculously handsome face of his. He was tall, dark, and as attractive as can be.

And he was putting on his jacket.

The lightbulb clicked on in Dawn's head just as her phone rang. It was Myesha. She poked in an earbud and strolled into the dining room before pushing the green button to answer the call.

"One second, Esha," she said, approaching Wayno and Juice as the two men were getting up. She tapped Wayno on the shoulder.

"What up?" he said.

"Where you headed to?"

"Do something for Juice."

"Can you take me to Walgreen's while you're out? I just need to grab some personal stuff. Won't take but a minute."

He agreed to give her a lift, and Dawn smiled before rushing out the door to grab her coat from her apartment. She didn't notice that Myesha was crying until she was going up the black-carpeted stairs.

"Girl, what's wrong?" Dawn said, so caught up in a swarm of fantasies featuring Wayno that she had forgotten all about Detroit Lenny's murder.

"Somebody killed Lenny," Myesha cried, "and Marshall's blaming it on you and Shawnna. He went to Detroit. I think he's coming back with some of their family. He's mad and his nose is broken and now his brother's dead. I don't know what he's about to do. All I know is he said he's coming back, and he was hot as fish grease when he said it. So be careful. You and Shawnna be careful. God, how did I get caught up in this? I promise, I will *never* fuck another nigga that's fucking one of my friends."

"I talked to Shawnna about a half hour ago," Dawn said. "I don't think she's mad at you anymore. It was really Lenny's fault all that shit went down. We didn't have nothing to do with him getting killed, though. Shawnna wasn't even out here, and I was in the house with my mama."

"Tell her I said hi."

Slipping into a full-length white leather coat, Dawn whisked back out of her apartment without even attempting to shout the hello. "I'll tell her," she said.

"Are we cool now?" Myesha asked.

"I never had a problem with you."

"Can you do me a favor and tell your sister I apologize? I'm not trying to be beefing with her. Especially when she hits like a fucking man. I've been in all kinds of fights, but never have I been hit so hard that I was literally put to sleep. That's some scary shit."

"Don't feel bad. She beat my ass last night too, and she knocked Mama out."

"Oh my God, are you serious?"

"As a heart attack," Dawn said. She was sauntering out the front door, and Wayno was right behind her. She swung her hips a little harder than usual as she began to strut down the stairs. It was just five degrees outside, the type of cold that grabbed at the bones of Chicago pedestrians, but the chill wasn't enough to stop Dawn from displaying her sexiest characteristics.

"Now I don't feel as bad," Myesha said. "Let me get my face cleaned up and get back out here with my fam. We're all here at my granny's house in K-Town. I'll hit you back later."

"Okay. Love you, bestie," Dawn said.

"Love you too."

They were approaching Wayno's long red Chevy Suburban. Although he had one arm cradled in a navy-blue sling, he still went out of his way to open the passenger door for her and help her inside.

She lifted her shoulders up around her ears and rubbed her hands together as he shut the door and headed around to the driver's side. He looked both ways before pulling open the driver door and climbing in, and she knew he was looking for signs of potential danger. She turned in her seat and did a little looking around of her own. He started the engine, moved a big black handgun from his waist to his lap, and leaned back in his seat.

"Let it warm up a minute," he said.

She thought: *God, why does his voice have to be so sexy?* Then: *What would Shawnna do in this situation? Would she just try to kiss him? Grab his crotch and tell him to drive to his place so they could fuck? What would Shawnna do?*

"You smell so good," Wayno said.

Dawn remembered hearing Lil Mark say the same thing to Shawnna at their birthday party last year, and she remembered Shawnna's reply verbatim, so she said it to Wayno.

"And I taste even better. If you doubt it I'll sit on your face and let you find out for yourself." She smiled nervously, but she was proud of herself for having the courage to voice such a slutty response.

"That don't even sound like some shit you would say. Who you learn that from? Shawnna or Myesha? It had to come from one of 'em."

"It came from me," she lied, and turned her head to look at him. He was smiling too. "Don't smile at me."

"Damn, I can't smile now?" he said.

"Not at me."

"Why not?"

"Because you know how long I've been after you. Because I feel like you think I'm ugly or something. Because you're fucking the same nasty hoe who fucked five bum-ass niggas in an abandoned building on Central Park. You better hope she don't have you pissing fire."

"That's what they made rubbers for."

"I'm saying, though - why fuck a hoe that's been passed around when you can have a bad-ass bitch like me?"

Wayno chuckled and shook his head. He sat forward, lowered the transmission into drive, and pulled off. "I love hoes," he said. "Hoes make the world go round. I know Tamia's reputation. That's why I strap up every time I put my dick in that pussy. And you're talking like she's my girlfriend. She ain't my bitch. I am single. Only reason I keep her around is because she sucks my dick all day. All I gotta do is pull this beg mu'fucka out. That's it."

"And she handles the rest," Dawn muttered discontentedly.

"Exactly," Wayno said. He paused. "Look back there and make sure we ain't being followed. Your pops thinks he's under surveillance by the Feds."

"Yeah, he told me. They took his picture." She looked back for a long moment. The closest vehicle she coils see rolling up the street behind them was a small white car two blocks back, and it turned down a side street four seconds later. "Nope. Nobody's following us."

"Keep checking."

"Keep checking," she mocked in her best Wayno impression. Then, in her own voice, she added, "You need to keep checking your penis to make sure it ain't fell off. That's what you really need to be checking. Since you got a thing for thots."

He laughed. "You too crazy."

"It's cool, my nigga," Dawn said. "It's cool. I see what I gotta do. I see what it's gonna take."

"What it's gon' take?"

"*Rape*. Ever been raped before?" She began to slide out of the trench coat, biting the middle of her lower lip, harnessing all her Shawnna vibes for one last leap of faith. "Huh, Wayno? Ever had a bitch just take that dick from you?"

"Don't get on no bullshit, Dawn."

"Oh, I'm most definitely on bullshit, Wayno." She tilted her seat back and undid her double-G belt buckle. "You see, I would grab that dick right now and jump on it, but I don't want us crashing. I'll tell you one thing, though: before we get back to the house, I'm getting me some good Wayno for Christmas. By will or by force, either way is fine with me."

He didn't say anything as she unbuttoned and unzipped her jeans. He might have grinned, but he didn't say a word. She peeled the jeans forward to her knees, then decided she would be better off going all the way and pushed her panties to her knees too.

"Look at all this good thickness," she said, rubbing her hands on her thighs. "This that cornbread, Wayno. That cornbread. And look at how fat my pussy is. Ooh, and it be so wet too. Look." She ran her middle finger down the shut lips of her pussy and then showed him the glistening moisture on her fingertip.

"Why do I feel like I'm sitting here with Shawnna?" Wayno said. He was having a hard time keeping his eyes on the road. He kept glancing between her legs and licking his lips. "I don't know why you're doing me like this. You know I work for your pops."

"Who *doesn't* work for my pops?

"I'm saying, though…"

"You're saying what? I'm eighteen. You know what that means? I'm grown as can fucking be. I'm grown as fuck, I'm thick as fuck, I'm independent as fuck, and I can count the number of niggas I've fucked on one hand. Put your finger in there and feel how tight it is."

The Suburban was rumbling down Homan Avenue. There weren't many Chicagoans loitering around the usual hangout spots. They passed Zaniyah's house, and Dawn saw a collection of shattered glass where Zaniya's minivan was usually parked. It was still early, just a quarter past seven.

Dawn commenced fingering herself. "Every time I play with my pussy," she said, in a voice you might hear from a phone sex operator, "I think about you fucking me. Every time

I look at videos on Pornhub or Xvideos, I look for dark-skinned niggas with dreadlocks, and I imagine… mmmm…I imagine it's you fucking me. Did you know that?"

Wayno was speechless. His eyes shifted from the road to her naked lower region and back to the road again. His tongue kept darting out and tracing his full lips, as if they were chapped and he was using his saliva to moisturize them. He was inhaling deeply through his nose. A bulge was growing in the crotch of his jeans, about two inches to the right of his gun.

"Yeah, you like that smell, don't you?" Dawn said, chuckling. She slid the middle and ring fingers of her right hand out of her pussy, thrust her pelvis forward, and smacked her wet fingertips on her hooded clit. "Good, clean pussy, Wayno. That's what you're smelling. That's what I got. You know how Homer Simpson likes to wrap his hands around Bart's neck to choke him? That's how this tight pussy will strangle that dick."

Sensing that he was close to the breaking point, she thumbed her jeans and panties down to her ankles and stepped out of them. She reclined the adjustable seat as far back as it could go and lifted her knees way up, holding her thighs wide open. She smacked her clitoris again.

"Do you eat pussy, Wayno?"

"Hell yeah I eat pussy," he said, keeping his eyes on the road now.

"When's the last time you ate some pussy?"

He shrugged. "It's been a while. I definitely didn't eat Tamia's."

"Would you eat mine?" Dawn shifted toward him, holding her left leg straight up so that the red bottom of her Louboutin boot almost touched the roof.

Wayno made a hasty right turn and an even hastier left turn, and suddenly they were in an alleyway. He parked.

"I didn't want to," he said, turning to her. "But you leave me no choice."

Wayno buried his tongue in her pussy, and she tangled her fingers in his dreads and forced his flickering tongue in deeper. He moved up to her clit and sucked on it. She moaned. He sucked harder; she moaned louder.

"Oh shit," she said breathlessly.

He hadn't been at it two minutes when her orgasm came, and it was a real screamer. It seized her, and she trembled fiercely. He ran the flat of his tongue up and down her pussy, then straightened it and poked it right into her asshole.

She gasped. She'd never had her asshole licked before. It felt good (hell, it felt *great!*), so she didn't say anything. She just moaned softly and let him do it. He went in deep. His long tongue waggled around inside of her. She toyed with her clit while he tongue fucked her virgin hole, and by the time his hungry mouth returned to her pussy she was ready for a second orgasm. This one was less intense, yet it lasted longer.

Seemingly content, Wayno moved back into his seat, his eyes glued to her glistening-wet pussy.

"Thank you so much," Dawn said, lowering her feet to the floor in front of her seat and leaning forward to pick up her jeans and panties. "You don't know how bad I needed that. It's been almost five months since I last had sex."

"What the fuck you mean 'thank you'?" Wayno said, and looked down at the frightening large bulge in the crotch of his jeans. "You better climb over to that back seat. Bart gotta get choked out before I pull off."

Chapter 16

The mood was fairly cheerful in Jah's hospital room, considering the fact that yesterday morning he'd been shot once in his upper left thigh, once in his right side, once in his left forearm, and twice in his left shoulder.

Jah was in a painkiller-induced slumber. A nurse came in at the start of every hour to wake him up and check on him. He would stay awake for twenty minutes or so, smiling and chatting with the family as much as he could, and then drift back off into dreamland.

It was 7:34 a.m., just twenty-six minutes until Jah's next wake-up, and Rell was in the chair closest to the left side of his brother's hospital bed. He was also drugged up, only his drug of choice was a powerful strain of Kush; he and Tamera had smoked two big blunts of it when they left out to grab breakfast about an hour ago.

She was in the chair next to Rell's. Her eyes were low and red. Her left hand was lost in a noisily crackling bag of barbecue-flavored Ruffles. Tirzah had just left to shower and change clothes at home - at least that was the reason she'd given Tamera. Rell believed the real reason Tirzah had left was because she'd overheard his phone conversation with Felicia Saunders, the mother of Jah's two-year-old daughter, Dora. Felicia was on her way to the hospital with Dora, and since Tirzah absolutely despised every woman Jah had ever slept with, she'd left the hospital. That's what Rell believed.

Rell was scrolling down his Facebook news feed. "They turned up at The Visionary Lounge last night," he said.

"I knoooow," Tamera whined. "We missed Jeezy *and* Tip. Why did Jah have to get shot on Christmas Eve morning? That's some straight up bullshit. I was looking forward to that party."

"We'll catch the next one."

"Look at Kev and Tara. They went to that party and stayed for no more than an hour, and they're over there sleeping better than Jah is."

It was true. Kev and Tara were out cold on the burgundy couch across from Jah's hospital bed. They were covered by a thick gray blanket Tara had brought from home, her on top of him.

"I'm just glad my li'l brother's okay," Rell said. He closed out the Facebook app and pocketed his phone. He had on a black hoodie, black sweatpants, and black Timbs. Although he wore a light smile, inside he felt as dark as his attire. Somebody had sent five bullets through his eighteen-year-old brother's body. Somebody was going to pay for that.

"A black Dodge Ram with Indiana plates," Tamera said thoughtfully. "I wonder if it's a stolen truck. Maybe whoever shot Jah stole that truck from somewhere in Indiana for the sole purpose of using it to do the shooting. Or am I thinking too hard?"

"Nobody can really say what happened as of now," Rell said. "All we know is that the truck was already riding up and down 16th Street before we even got back from Cali. Wayno saw it driving through the snowstorm Friday night. He saw three niggas in it, and Lil Mark - shit, you know how Lil Mark get down - he almost shot the truck up after they saw it the third time."

"Wish he would have done it."

"Wayno saw their faces. He didn't recognize either of them."

"Maybe they're *from* Indiana."

"They might be. I don't know. What I do know is there weren't three guys in there when the driver started shooting. I saw the driver. He was older, probably in his forties or late thirties."

"Then it wasn't Jamal's brother," Tamera said, tilting the bag upside down and dumping the remaining crumbs in her mouth. "James is only a few years older than Jamal. Think he's the same age as Jah."

Jamal was a sixteen-year-old who'd been murdered this past Thursday, shot dead on the corner of 15th Street and Trumbull Avenue. His murder had come shortly after he'd threatened the lives of Jah and Tirzah for allegedly jumping his sister, Mila Cushenberry. It was actually Tirzah and Tamera who'd assaulted Mila - quite brutally, in fact - but none of that had mattered to Jah. Once he had learned that Jamal was not only making death threats on social media but also asking the guys in North Lawndale for a gun, Jah popped up on Trumbull Avenue and whacked the kid before the kid could whack him. Everyone suspected Jah of being Jamal's killer, but no one knew for certain, and those who'd witnessed the murder weren't talking. Especially since Styro, an older cat from the neighborhood, had allegedly given up Jah's name to two homicide detectives Friday morning and was found riddled with bullets on 16th Street that same night.

"It might not even be connected to Jamal," Rell said.

"But it might be," Tamera said.

"I got a feeling it is."

"Nobody at Mila's house has a pickup truck."

"Could've been a cousin or an uncle."

"True."

"I'll find whoever did it. Believe me, it won't be long before I have that old fuck stretched out in a casket right next to Jamal."

Tamera turned to him and smiled. "Are you mad again?"

"Mad ain't the word."

"Well, whatever you were when we got home last night."

"I don't think I'm that upset. Jah was in surgery then. I didn't know if he would make it. I've never been so upset in my life. I was steaming."

"I wish I could bottle that emotion." Her smile widened an inch. "I would mass produce whatever chemical that is and make you drink a cup of it every night before we go to bed. The way you put it down on that couch... Mmm. I just about *died*."

Rell bit his bottom lip and smiled around the teeth. She stood up to toss her empty chip bag in the rash, and he smacked her on the seat of her snug-fitting sweatpants. They were pink with black leather stripes running down the sides. The hooded sweater was pink with a black leather rectangle on the chest. Her pink Timbs even had pink shoestrings. She'd purchased the outfit herself, but he knew she was only wearing it to match the pink lambskin Chanel bag he'd given her for Christmas.

She rinsed her greasy fingers off in the bathroom sink and returned to her seat. "Can you believe it's actually Christmas already?" she said.

"I know, right?" he said.

"We actually met on Christmas morning last year. Technically, it's our first anniversary of being together."

"Damn." Rell thought about it. "You're right. It *was* Christmas."

"Do you remember how we met?" Tamera asked.

"Of course, I remember."

"How did we meet?" She was obviously testing him, thinking he actually did not remember. She shifted toward him, twisting open a Snapple drink and taking a swig from it. "Tell me, Rell. How did we meet?"

"Let's see, uh… My daddy told me to collect the rent in that apartment building he owned on Douglas and Homan. He said, 'Be careful, son. You got Tamera and that other Lyon girl down there, and they are truly some lions. They will pounce on you so fast. Have you walking down the aisle before you know it.' And wouldn't you know it? One of 'em pounced on me, the other one pounced on my brother, and *both* of our dumb asses walked down the aisle."

She punched him on the shoulder and gave an amused smile. "That is not what the hell he said. Big man knew me better than a lot of people in that building knew me. If he was here today he would tell you how long it had been since I was last with a man before you came along."

"I was just talkin' shit," Rell said. He raised her right hand to his mouth and put a soft, lasting kiss just behind the dark knuckles. "I remember knocking on your door. I remember the door opening, and I remember seeing your sexy-ass face before you slammed the door closed."

Tamera giggled. "I was nervous."

"You were beautiful," Rell said seriously. "And you're even more beautiful every time I look at you. Every morning I wake up next to you. You're the best thing that ever happened to me. You made me appreciate black women in a whole 'nother way. I feel like I wasn't even me until I met you." He gave the back of her hand another long kiss. "I will *always* love you. Unconditionally. That's a promise I can keep."

There were tears of joy in Tamera's eyes. She had on a big Colgate smile, and she was leaning into him. "That was…" She seemed to consider her words as she wristed the tears away. "It was exactly what I needed to hear. You always say the right things at the right time. And you mean it - that's what's so sweet about you. You're always so…"

"Sincere?" Rell offered, and she punched his shoulder again, because Sincere Jerrell Owens was his name.

"Real smart, jackass," she said, leaning toward him.

He leaned toward her, and their lips met at the halfway mark. He tasted the barbecue Ruffles and the Snapple on her tongue. He knew without a doubt that the passion in her kiss was a direct result of his lover's reply to her meaningful question a moment ago. He'd meant every heartfelt word. Tamera was a dream come true. She was a beautiful black woman with high cheekbones and soft, thick lips. She hadn't worked a day job ever since they first got together last year, and he didn't mind if it stayed that way. He had gotten his real estate license in June of this year, and he now owned a total of seven houses. That didn't include the apartment building and eight houses his father had left to him and Jah. He was financially stable, and what was his was hers. She was a worthy housewife who took care of home, the ultimate voice behind a lot of his most important decisions, the rock that held him in place when the winds of life's frequent storms tried to blow him away.

Their mouths separated. He cracked open his own beverage - a pineapple Fanta soda - and downed a third of it. "Got chips all in my mouth," he said, and chuckled.

"Shut up."

"You heard from Shawnna?"

"I sent her a text. She ain't hit me back yet." Tamera pulled out her iPhone. "You know I can't wait to hear about what happened between her and Myesha. Everybody on Facebook is talking about that. They say she went there and cleaned house."

"Her crazy ass," Rell said.

Just then, someone knocked at the door and at the same time pushed it open. It was Felicia. She had Dora on one hip and an oversize diaper bag knocking against the other.

"Uncle Rell!" Dora screamed excitedly, only it came out *Unca Well*. She slipped down from her mother's hip, losing her coat in the process, and came streaking toward Rell. "Merry Christmas, Uncle Rell! I missed you!"

Kev, Tara, and Jah woke up instantly.

"Uncle Rell," Dora said as she climbed him like a ladder and took a seat on his knee, "did you get me that stupid egg for Christmas? Because my mama said you gave it to me and I told her you didn't."

"You mean the Hatchimal?" Rell said, laughing.

Dora nodded. "It's stupid. It don't open."

The others joined in on the laughter. Tara headed into the bathroom. Jah held down the button that raised the head-end of his bed, and it lifted with a low pneumatic buzz.

"Merry Christmas, Dora," Jah muttered weakly.

Dora whipped her head around to look at Jah, and she brought both of her hands up to cover her nose and mouth. "Merry Christmas, Daddy," she said from behind her little brown hands. "Why you sick?"

All eyes went to Felicia, who had the guiltiest expression on her face as she sat down in the hair next to Tamera's. "I know, I know," she said, groaning inwardly. "I told her that to keep her from climbing all over you."

"I'm not sick, Dora," Jah said. "I just got hurt."

"Are you sure?" Dora asked tentatively.

"Absolutely."

"Okay," Dora said, sounding leery still. She slowly lowered her hands to her lap, tilted her head up, and sniffed at the air, as if she would be able to smell the sickness if it was there.

More laughs around the room.

"You gotta rub the egg," Rell said, and Dora turned back to him. "You gotta rub it and hold it to make it hatch."

Dora shook her head, pouting. She folded her arms over her chest. "I rubbed it. I hugged it. I sat on it. I threw it down the stairs. It's stupid. You got me a stupid toy, Uncle Rell. A stupid broke toy. Thanks a lot."

Felicia said, "Did either of y'all see those two police officers standing out there?"

"Police officers?" Rell looked at Felicia.

She nodded just as the door crept open. A middle-aged nurse led in two white men with CPD badges embroidered on their shirts and clipped to their waists. They were large and intimidating, like two John Cenas, and their names were stitched over the cloth badges on their shirts: Detective J.W. Bryant and Detective R. Milam. *Homicide*

"Jahlil Owens?" Milam said, holding an ink pen in one hand and a small yellow notepad in the other. "Mind if we ask you a few questions?"

Jah didn't say a word.

Detective Bryant glanced around the room. "Can you all step out into the hall and give us a minute with Jahlil?"

"Is he under arrest?" Rell said, getting up.

Tamera raised her iPhone and went live on Facebook. The detectives scowled at her and turned their eyes back to the wounded man they'd come to question.

"Jahlil," Milam said, "can you tell us where you were on the night of Thursday, December twenty-second?"

Jah stared silently at the two detectives; his expression unreadable.

Detective Bryant took two steps forward. Then a third. He was eyeing Rell. "Maybe you can help us out," he said. "We're investigating the murder of sixteen-year-old Jamal Cushenberry. Some coward put five bullets in his head. You heard anything about it? Because we had a guy tell us that Jahlil was rumored to be the shooter, and now that guy is also dead. He was gunned down two nights ago on 16th and Spaulding. Christopher Walsh was his name. You might've known him as Styro."

"We're just trying to get all this cleared up," Milam said, his calculating eyes fixed on Jah. "Figure out what's going on. Maybe you can start off by telling us who fired the weapon that landed you here in Northwestern Memorial in the first place. It may be connected to the other shootings."

Jahlil Owens pressed the button that made the head of his bed flat again. He shut his eyes and kept his lips sealed.

"Have it your way," Milam said, and pocketed his notepad and ink pen. "We will be seeing you soon, Mr. Owens."

"Count on it," Bryant added.

As the two detectives turned to leave, Dora flipped them off with two ring fingers. Everybody else made similar gestures - using the correct fingers, of course.

King Rio

Chapter 17

The kitchen was filled with the wonderful smells of oven-baked turkey, collard greens, mac and cheese, pinto beans, string beans, pumpkin pies, and a host of other delicious foods, many of which had been prepared by the woman who'd given birth to Bubbles nearly three decades ago.

They had loaded all of Bubbles and Ra'Mya's Christmas gifts into the Benz and Shawnna's Escalade (Juice had a spare key to the SUV), and Juice had tailed the Benz to "her place," while Ra'Mya talked his ear off in the passenger's seat. Tamia had ridden with Bubbles, probably to take another shot at getting the loan she'd been pestering Bubbles about since before Wayno and Dawn had left.

It was a big kitchen with shiny steel objects: fridge, double-basin sink, dishwasher, a stove that looked like it belonged in the kitchen of a restaurant. Bubbles and her sister, Kisha, who had driven in from Indianapolis with her four kids in tow, were bustling around the kitchen, finishing up the cooking their dear old Mama T (that's what they called her) had started. Juice and Mama T were sitting at the table, him texting Wayno to see where he and Dawn were at, her dabbing sweat from her brow with a tissue and smoking a Newport cigarette she'd stolen from Kisha's purse.

When he looked up from his smartphone, Mama T was peering at him through a haze of drifting smoke. Juice noticed there was a slight scratch on her left cheek. She was a pretty little lady with a nice smile - perfect white teeth - and a great cloud of gray-black hair. Her clothes were moderately expensive, and she had on an apron. "So how long you plan on stickin' my daughter before you come on with the come on?" She puffed on her cigarette as she asked the surprisingly hilarious question.

"*Mama!*" Bubbles shrieked, her head snapping around to regard Mama T with that signature squirt.

Kisha burst out laughing. So did Juice.

"I'm just talkin' to the man," Mama T said. "You keep your eyes in that damn pot, Kita. Them greens should be 'bout done. While you all over here in my mouth. Kisha, stir that spaghetti."

"Yeah, what she said." Juice nodded his head, grinning. "All over here in her mouth. Worry about what's on that stove."

"Really, Juice?" Bubbles said. "You on her side?" She pointed a big steel spoon at him. "Don't let her hype you up. You'll be *"stickin'"* - she made quotation marks with the first and second fingers of her hands - "your damned self tonight. 'Stickin' your hand. Palmela Handerson."

Mama T threw her head back and cackled. Her top teeth came down and clacked against the bottom teeth while her mouth was wide open, and suddenly Juice knew why they were so impossibly white. They were fakes. Man-made teeth. The kind you'd find in a glass of water on your grandma's bed-table, the cuspids looking like big white blocks, the canine teeth looking like vampire fangs sunk in the improbable pink plastic gums. She slapped her hand over her mouth, and he knew she was putting her tongue to work to get the dental malfunction under control. She was still laughing, and, having witnessed the dental malfunctioning, Juice and her daughters were also cracking up. Tendrils of smoke were emanating from her nose.

The laughter was beginning to die down when Juice's cell phone rang. It was Wayno hitting him back. He stood up, walked to the Formica-topped service island in the middle of the kitchen, and answered while peeling the saran wrap off a large bowl of homemade chocolate chip cookies.

"Yo," he said, his voice distorted by the soft cookie he was biting into.

"I just cleaned those shirts. Burn me up right quick," Wayno said.

"Yup," Juice said, and ended the call. He dug in his pocket, pulled out a prepaid Virgin Mobile flip phone he'd purchased at a gas station yesterday, and dialed one of the only two numbers saved in the contacts. It was his burner phone, the phone he used to talk business. He usually bought a new one every two or three weeks, and he required Wayno to get a new one at least once a month. The "shirts" Wayno had mentioned were kilos of cocaine. Following the shooting yesterday morning, he had dropped off twenty bricks to an aunt of Wayno's in the East Garfield Park neighborhood.

"Dough snatched 'em all up," Wayno said.

"Please tell me you dropped my daughter back off before you went and took care of that business," Juice said.

"I couldn't do that."

Juice clenched his teeth. "Why not?"

"Because I only got one arm to work with and Dough just laid these three heavy-ass duffel bags on me. I can't run all this bread through the money machines by myself. I tried calling Kev to come and help me but him and Rell was all paranoid and shit."

"Paranoid about what?"

"These same two detectives. They just came to Jah's hospital room, asking about the shit with Jamal. Ain't Tamera your friend on Facebook? You can see the whole video on her page. She recorded the whole thing live. Jah laid down and closed his eyes. I laughed my ass off when I saw that video."

It hardly took Juice five seconds to get to the video on Tamera's page. He let it play without sound. He would listen to it when he finished talking to Wayno.

Besides, just hearing about the two homicide detectives again had him on edge, very near panic. His heart was now racing so fast, he couldn't detect the individual beats; it seemed to be just a steady hand hum in his chest and high in his neck, below the points of his jaw. If those two cops had stumbled upon him before he'd delivered the twenty kilos to Wayno's aunt, he would have been like Jeff Fort, or Larry Hoover. There wouldn't have been a chance in the world of getting out of prison again.

I'm all good, he thought. *It didn't happen.*

No. But he could see himself lying there in that prison cell all the same, and with hellish clarity. Lying there with only a pile of dog-eared car magazines for company. Lying there and waiting decades for a heart attack or some form of cancer to come along and put him out of his misery. And how long would that take? Would it be thirty years? Fifty? Only ten?

"Man," Wayno said, "I'm starting to think those two pigs got it out for the whole gang. They keep pulling me over. They took pictures of you. Now they done started fuckin with Jah and Rell. That's a lot, big homie. Now I'm sitting here with damn near half a milli in cash, can't even get no assistance 'cause you don't want nobody else touching the money. You want me to just bring this shit to you? Or do you want Dawn to help me put it all through this money machine? Let me know what you want me to do."

"Just bring it to me."

"In Lake Forest?'

"Yeah. Just bring it out here. I'll count it myself." Juice clamped a hand over his eyes. "I want you to get out of Chicago until your wrist heals up. It's too hot in the hood anyway. I'll pay for the trip. Go to Jamaica, or Hawaii if that's where you wanna go. Tell Rell to go with you."

"Rell ain't going nowhere until he finds whoever shot his li'l brother. You know it like I know it. I'll tell him, though. If that's what you want me to tell him, then that's what I'll do."

"I'll talk to him. You just get out of town," Juice said. He returned to his seat at the table, put his bitten cookie on a napkin because he no longer craved for it, and passed a nervously shocking hand across his forehead.

"You really want me to leave?" Wayno said. "Why would you want me to leave when I'm your only right hand? Who you gonna trust to run this shit while I'm gone?"

"Let me worry about that," Juice muttered, and then he did a strange thing - strange, at least, for him, a man who was ordinarily so easy and self-assured. He got up, walked into the living room, and looked out through the blinds, as if afraid he had been followed.

"I need the address," Wayno said.

"What address?"

"To the house in Lake Forest. You know I ain't been there. Dawn said she ain't been there, either. You and Bubbles act like it's a top secret hideout or some shit."

Juice paused, thinking about DEA and FBI agents in SWAT gear. "Look, just give the duffels to Dawn. Tell her to drive that shit out here to me. What I want you to do is shut down shop. I don't want a gram moving in Holy city for the next forty-eight hours, and if another body drops out there I'm raising hell. Take ten Gs out of that money, close down shop, give Lil Mark a new burner phone and this number, then get on a fucking plane and go. Don't even stop by your spot to pack. Just get to the airport and get the fuck out of Chicago."

"Are you seriously thinking about putting Lil Mark in char——"

Juice flipped the phone shut. For a moment he just stood there at the living room window, the flip phone in a loose fist at his side, his iPhone in the hand he was fingering the blinds open with.

Another hellish vision came to him: calling Bubbles collect from prison and having his call answered by Wayno. "I don't know how to tell you this, big homie," Wayno would say, while Bubbles lay naked in bed with him, "but me and Bubbles, uhh…we're engaged. And I'd appreciate it if you stopped calling this number." He hated to think such a thing about the two most loyal people he had in his life at the moment, but he'd seen it happen to a thousand men in prison. The men in Stateville had even given it a name: The Jody factor. As in Tyrese Gibson's character in the movie *Baby Boy*.

"Juice," Bubbles said, startling him out of his reverie. She was right up on him, peering around his shoulder - his shoulder was too high for her to peer over it - to see what he was staring at outside.

He put the phones in his pockets, turned around to face her, and planted his hands on her hips. She had on white leggings and a white Chicago Cubs 2016 World Series Champions T-shirt. He kissed her lips and slid his hands around to her big spherical gluteus maximus.

"You okay?" she asked.

"I'm okay," he said.

"You sure?"

"I'm sure." Juice nodded.

"You look worried."

"You look sexy." He squeezed. "*Feel* sexy."

"Juice, I'm serious. What's going on? Why are you standing here looking out my living room window? Has something happened?"

He stared into her sweet brown eyes and saw that she was trying to read his thoughts. He rubbed her ass from where it began at her lower back to where it ended at the rear of her thighs and decided it had to be twice as full and round as Serena's. Probably twice as soft, too; his fingers sunk into the feather-soft flesh of it.

"Yeah," he said, after a moment. "Remember the pigs in the black Challenger? The ones that took pictures of us?"

"How could I forget?"

"Well, they just showed up in Jah's hospital room, asking about Jamal's murder. And Wayno done been pulled over a few times by the same two cops. That shit got me thinking. What if we're all under investigation? It can't be a coincidence that they keep showing up where we're at. And the fact that I just got a thousand fucking kilos from your ex-sugar daddy isn't making it any better."

"A *thousand*?"

He nodded. 'A thousand. And I just sold twenty of 'em to Grindo for twenty-two a piece. Your guy only wants ten G's a brick, so that's two hundred thousand for him and two forty for me."

"You need to start keeping me in the loop about these things. There isn't much I can say when you don't let me in on it till the last minute," Bubbles snapped at him. But her eyes were not snappish; they were soft, thinking, strategizing. "Okay, so the two cops are becoming a problem. What more do you know about them?"

"All I know is they're homicide detectives, and their names are Bryant and Milam. One of 'em is the one who killed Zo earlier this year."

"If they're homicide detectives, then it all makes perfect sense. Jah killed Jamal; Styro pretty much told them that much, right? They want Jah for the murder, and Jah got shot right in front of your house on Drake. That's why they were there snapping pictures when we pulled up last night. And the only reason they keep pulling Wayno over is because they've probably been seeing a lot of the younger guys riding in that hot-ass red Suburban with him. You need to just keep your distance from him and Jah for a while. And make Wayno trade in that Suburban." She concluded her strategy with a kiss to his chin.

Juice thrust out his bottom lip and nodded. "All right," he said. Now he felt perfectly willing to entrust the leadership of the whole matter to her. "All right. I already told Wayno to leave, to go on a vacation. I'm about to have Dawn bring me that cash."

"Then just fall back from everything. Let somebody else take your place the organization." She took a step back, and suddenly she became the worried one. "Oh shit. I almost forgot why I came in here to get you in the first place. My girl Shay - you know her, she's Bankroll Reese's assistant - she just called and said you need to call and talk to Shawnna. I guess her and Reese got into it over him getting Myesha pregnant. Shawnna flipped out and started shooting."

Chapter 18

Shawnna smiled - a malicious smile full of evil innocence. She was sitting next to Reese in the back seat of his Bentley SUV, holding a pickle up in front of her mouth and getting ready to bite into it as Chubb started the engine.

"You're so fucking crazy," Reese said. He was hunched forward, his eyes boring into her. "You could've shot me, Shawnna. You could've fucking *killed* me."

"I am not crazy," she said, slowly and haltingly. "You got my best friend pregnant, behind my back. I lost my best friend because of you. You lied and told me I was your one and only, and the whole time you and Myesha were fucking behind my back. I believe that makes you and her the crazy ones. I'm the psychiatrist, if anything. I gave you two nasty bitches the counseling y'all really needed. Now if you don't want to be faithful to me, let me know that, and I'll gladly leave you alone. If you *do* want to be with me, then you're going to be faithful to me. It's as simple as that."

"Crazy-ass bitch," he muttered through clenched teeth.

"Nasty-ass nigga," she countered with her malicious smile. "Don't get mad at me for your fuck-up."

"You put twenty holes in my goddamn headboard."

"Twenty-three, actually." She took a bite out of the pickle, chewed it up, and swallowed. "I counted the holes. You're lucky I didn't empty both clips. I have a doctor's appointment tomorrow to find out the sex of this baby, and if he finds any purple little monsters dancing around in my ovaries, I'm shooting *at* you instead of over your head next time."

"What the fuck are you talking about? What the fuck is up with these purple goddamn monsters?" he moved forward in his roomy seat as he could look at his driver. "You hear this shit?"

Chubb chuckled, shook his head, and hit the heels of his hands on the steering wheel. He was driving out the front gate, which was already swinging shut behind them. Shay was in the passenger's seat, earbuds closing her off from the drama as she jammed out to some unknown tunes while replying to emails, text messages, and social media comments.

"You know what I mean," Shawnna said to Reese. "I don't mean actual monsters. I'm talking about diseases. I've never had an STD and I don't plan on having any in the future. Especially not when I'm pregnant. You're going to respect my body, Reese. I mean that from the bottom of my heart. I love myself way too much to let a nigga burn my pussy up. If you don't want to be faithful to me, then I don't want to be with you."

Reese sat back and exhaled loudly. He tilted his head back on the headrest. She could see the muscles in his jaw working as he repeatedly clenched and unclenched his teeth. He balled his hands into fists in his lap. Shawnna watched him cautiously, feeling a trickle of unease now. Maybe she had pushed him to his breaking point. Maybe he was considering the idea of fucking her up in the back seat of his sexy red Bentley Bentayga. Maybe he was about to drop her off on Drake Avenue and never contact her again.

All of a sudden, her heart began to ache. Tears burst from her eyes and cascaded down her cheeks. *Goddamn hormones,* she thought morosely. *Should be called WHORE-MOANS, because that's what they are.* She wanted to laugh at the thought, or voice it, but all she could do was sit there with tears racing down her face like a pair of pro snowboarders at an X-Games event, holding up a pickle she had only taken three bites out of, wondering if she had just lost her unborn child's father.

He looked at her, saw that she was crying, and let out another loud breath. "I apologize, a'ight?" he said. "I'm man enough to admit when I'm wrong, and I know I was wrong for cheating. Okay? I don't wanna lose you, Shawnna. I can't even sit here and act like I'm mad at you for what you did without being mad at my damn self for giving you a reason to do what you did. I cheated, I know I was wrong, and I'll never do it again."

There was a pure sincerity in his eyes and in his words that told her he was telling the truth. He looked to her amazingly as he had when she'd first seen him at a high school basketball game in their sophomore year - sitting on the bench, his knees somewhere up around his ears, his hands on their narrow wrists dangling between his athletic legs. Only then he had been wearing basketball shorts and a towel slung around his neck, and now he was in a Balmain sweater and jeans. He had started in many games, she remembered finally, because his older half-brother, Rodney "Hot Rod" Earl, had been drafted straight to the NBA from high school. And because he was good.

"Don't cry, baby," Reese said, and fingered the tears off her face. He put his arm around Shawnna and smiled. "No more cheating, okay? No threat of purple monsters over here."

"Don't get beat up," she mock-growled, and threw a light punch at his midsection.

Outside, the wind whooshed around the SUV, rocking it a little as Chubb drove into the windy city. The murky light of dawn had changed; from a dull orange it had gone to a bright, almost blinding yellow that glared off the windows of the buildings they passed and made both Chubb and Shay lower their sun visors. The sun was a great ball of yellow on the horizon. Shawnna wondered how it could be so bone-chillingly cold when the sun was beaming so harshly. Chubb turned on the radio and hummed along to a Chance the Rapper song. Shawnna relaxed with Reese's arm around her - she had seen more of him in the last seven days then she had all year, it seemed, and she was very pleased to discover that she liked it. She had never been pregnant before, either, and she had to keep reminding herself that her baby's father was a millionaire, her baby's father was a *multi*millionaire. Thousands should be so lucky.

Then her cell phone rang in her purse and she stopped thinking about her baby's rich father for a moment, though her head stayed on his shoulder as she dug the phone out and answered her dad's call.

"You okay?" Juice asked immediately.

"Well, Merry Christmas to you too, father," she said, and bit a small chunk out of the pickle.

"Merry Christmas, Shawnna. Now tell me what went on between you and Reese this morning."

"Wow. Word travels fast." She sucked on the open top of the pickle to get some of the peppermint in her mouth. "We had a little argument. That's all it was. A disagreement. We got it under control."

"What did you do?"

"Threw some stuff."

"I heard you threw some bullets."

Shawnna snickered. "Yeah. I didn't shoot *him*, though. Just the headboard."

"You gotta calm down. I got cops taking pictures of me and Bubbles, I just damn near got whacked yesterday, and every time I look up it's something else with you. Can you please relax until you push that baby out? That's all I'm asking, Shawnna."

"I'll be good from now on, Daddy. I just needed to get some stuff off my chest," Shawnna said, really meaning it. She had been thinking about her baby's well-being ever since she'd tossed the two smoking guns into Reese's bedroom closet. She was tripping, and she had to do better.

"That's all I'm asking," Juice replied.

"Are you at home?"

"Nah, I'm out here with Bubbles."

"At her house in Lake Forest?"

"Yeah. I drove your truck out here too."

"Thanks for asking first," Shawnna said sarcastically. "Is Bubbles cooking? And is Dawn there with you?

"Bubbles and her mom cooked. There's enough for every-body, in case you and Reese wanna come through. Dawn's at home, but she's about to come out here with us."

"Let me call her right quick."

"All right. Call me back." Juice hung up.

Shawnna dialed her sister's phone, got no answer, and left a scathing voicemail: "Don't get beat up again, bitch. I know you saw me calling. What did you do, go on Backpage and hire yourself a man for Christmas? Call me back ASAP or I'm breaking your phone *and* your neck. Bitch."

She hung up, lifted her head from Reese's shoulder, and smiled at him. There was no evil innocence in this smile, just love and happiness. An Al Green smile. She kissed him on the side of his mouth.

"Shawnna," he said, "you're missing some screws."

"It might just be that I need to get screwed," she said

"So what's the play?"

"I just want to stop by my dad's apartment to get my pre-sents from under the tree. I know he got me some stuff I really wanted, or at least I hope he did."

"Then what?" Reese asked. A face-trembling yawn sepa-rated his jaws and stretched his mouth open. "Because I ain't had a blink of sleep. No thanks to you, I'm falling right into *your* bed - since you fucked mine all up."

"I'm sorry." She pecked his cheek again. "You can get in my bed and stay there as long as you want. But can we go somewhere and have breakfast first? Your daughter is hungry, and so is her mom."

He knitted his brows. "Thought you said you're going in tomorrow to learn the sex of the baby?"

"Yeah, but I want a girl, so I'm going to speak it into existence."

"We're having a boy." Reese let out a sleepy chuckle. "Who did you just cuss out on the phone?"

"Muy lame-ass twin. She only ignores my calls when she's with a man, and the bitch ain't got no man. She's too scared to give it up without having me there to hype her up to do it. Even if it's somebody she really likes. She has the hugest crush on Wayno, but she ain't got the guts to give him some o' dat Becky."

Chapter 19

"Wayno…mmm…yeah…yeah…" Dawn wasn't normally so vocal during sex, but Wayno know what he was doing. He was behind her, holding her left hip in a firm grip while she bent over with her elbows on the dining table in her father's first-floor apartment.

There were rubber-band stacks of cash piled high on the table - $440,000 in all, but to Dawn it looked like $5 million. She had never seen so much cash. It was as if someone had emptied a bank vault onto the table.

Her jeans and panties were pooled around her ankles. Her iPhone lay screen-up between her forearms. She'd ignored Shawnna's call five seconds ago. It felt like Wayno's dick was on the verge of busting *through* her uterus, but it was a good feeling. Although it did hurt a little, it gave her ten times as much pleasure. Her pussy made wet sloshing noises as it con-tracted around his thick veiny phallus. Wayno was fucking her mercilessly, and she was enjoying every minute of it.

This was round two. He had fucked her in the back seat of his Suburban until tears had threatened to spill from her eyes. They had used protection in the Suburban, but there was no rubber sleeve on his dick now. She thought of how heavy with semen his condom had been when she'd slid it off his flaccid penis to throw it out the SUV window. Any man who released that much cum in a single orgasm was bound to get a girl preg-nant if protective measures weren't taken. What if *she* got pregnant? She wasn't looking to have a baby anytime soon, but she couldn't deny how cool it would be for her and Shawnna to have children around the same time. And to have Wayno as her baby's father was a definite plus.

About five minutes later, his fingers tightened on her hip, his thrusts became more urgent, and he let out a throaty moan of his own. "Here it go," he said. "Here it come."

"Cum in me, Wayno... Cum in me," Dawn pleaded, lacing her fingers together as if she was in prayer. Maybe her subconscious was praying for the painfully pleasureful vaginal pounding to finally come to an end (they'd been at it almost twenty minutes). Or maybe it was the baby her subconscious was praying for. Or maybe both.

"You want it in you?" Wayno asked aggressively.

"Yes...mmmm...yes," Dawn said

"You want this nut in you?"

"Yes...give it to me."

"There it go. There it go." He thrust forward, filling her completely. She could actually feel the hot gush of semen blasting out of him. "Give it that grip. Give Bart that chokehold."

Dawn tightened her vaginal muscles as much as she could. She was no expert on Kegel exercise, but she had taught herself how to flex those inner muscles after reading about Kegels online.

"That's it. That's it right there," Wayno said, and smacked his hand on her meaty left buttock. His dick was jerking around inside of her, still spewing its seed.

Right at that moment, the front door unlocked and flew open.

Dawn gasped and looked up to find Shawnna and Reese walking into the apartment. She reached down and snatched up her panties and jeans, but it was too late. She was busted. Shawnna was looking right at her.

"You dirty hoe," Shawnna said, and she was smiling. "Whose money is that? And why are y'all fucking on Daddy's dining room table? That's just nasty."

Wayno stroked the last few globs of thick white semen out of his dick, and they hit the glossy hardwood floor with loud splats. As Chubb and the skinny girl who followed Reese around everywhere walked in behind Reese and Shawnna. Reese began to laugh.

Dawn watched her sister's boyfriend laugh his gaspy hee-hawing laugh. He laughed so hard he finally had to lean over and put his hands on his knees, so hard Chubb and the skinny girl - Dawn remembered her name now, it was Shay - looked into the dining room to see what was so funny, and when they saw (Dawn was struggling to get the tight jeans up over her big butt, and Wayno was next to her with his erection tenting his boxers as he lifted his own jeans), they laughed, too. They all stood around in the open doorway and laughed at Dawn and Wayno, and Dawn forgot how much she wanted a baby. What she wanted now was to sling her iPhone and see if she could hit Shawnna in the face with it. She found she was more curious on this subject than on any other which had engaged her attention over the last several months, including the subject of her own involuntary celibacy.

"Y'all ever heard of knocking?" Dawn said bitterly.

Shawnna held up a keyring. "I got the keys, the keys, the keys," she sing merrily, strolling into the dining room. She looked at the small puddles of semen on the floor with a grimace of disgust. When she looked up, Dawn and Wayno were taking the bundles of cash off the table and placing them inside a large black duffel bag.

"Help us put all this money back in these duffel bags," Dawn said, because with Wayno's right arm cradled in a sling it would take them longer to refill the bags than she was willing to spend here with her bipolar twin. "It's Daddy's money. I gotta take it to him."

Reluctantly, Shawnna picked up an empty duffel and lent her help. Shay asked if she could use the bathroom and Dawn gave her directions: up the hall, second door on the left.

"Damn," Reese said, stepping up to the table. "Some birds landed? Where all this bread come from?"

"Worry about your own money, please," Dawn said. "You got more than enough of it."

"Ain't no such thing as enough money." He shut the front door, turned back to the dining room, and yawned. He looked tired, like maybe he hadn't slept last night. He stood leaning in the doorway between the living room and the dining room, practically asleep on his feet, Balmain jacket, sweater, and jeans, all as red as his Gucci sneaks.

Dawn moved close to Shawnna and gave her evil twin a nudge. "Myesha called me a little while ago. She's at her granny's house over on Kilpatrick. She was crying and all, asking me to talk you into forgiving her."

"I'll kill that bitch *and* Patrick," Shawnna muttered indifferently. "What's with all this money?"

"I don't know. Wayno gave Grindo two cardboard boxes, and Grindo gave us these duffel bags. Daddy wants us to bring it all to him in Lake Forest, and he wants Wayno to leave town."

"To Jamaica," Wayno said, stuffing a bundle of hundreds into the left-hand pocket of his jeans. "He gave me ten racks and told me to disappear for a while, until my wrist heals up. I'll probably just stay until the end of January. I ain't been out of Chicago in years. It'll be good for me."

"Why leave, though?" Shawnna asked.

"Because," Wayno said, "these two punk-ass police keep fucking with us, and they got the big homie worried. He's taking precautions, that's all. Taking control of the situation. I can't knock his thinking. Shit, he's the chief. I gotta go with whatever he say anyway. But I understand this play. We got too much going down out here. Way, way too much. Bodies dropping every day. Last night, we had about twenty cop cars riding up and down 16th, and a nigga still ended up gettin whacked. That nigga you got into it with."

Shawnna smirked. "Yeah, that's crazy," she said.

"*You're* crazy," Dawn corrected.

They finished bagging the money, and Dawn cleaned up the dick droppings. It was 10:00 a.m., cold outside but warm in the apartment, and Dawn could feel the cum beginning to slowly seep out onto the crotch of her panties. She ruminated about going to Jamaica with Wayno when she and Shawnna went to the Christmas tree to open their gifts. The boys stayed in the dining room, and so did the assistant.

High-end purses, shoes, coats, and outfits; diamond earrings, necklaces, rings, and watches; twin shoe boxes full of hundred-dollar bills - Juice had spoiled them this Christmas. They kneeled around the tree with delightful expressions on their identical faces, no longer eighteen but a decade younger, smiling and ahh'ing and ooh'ing as they had when they were just little girls.

Dawn had meant to mention the warning Myesha had given her about Marshall but caught up in the childish excitement this Christmas induced, she forgot all about it.

King Rio

Chapter 20

Marshall's sixty-two-year-old father, Leonard "Big Lenny" Green Sr., was standing tall in front of the living room television. Big Lenny was wearing his biballs with a collared shirt beneath, a shirt that looked as if it had once been red but was now faded to a no-account salmon by dozens or hundreds of washings, and beneath the collared shirt was the round top of a cotton undershirt, and this shirt was clean but the color of old ivory instead of its original white because Mrs. Green's motto, often spoken and shouted at the men of the Green family, was this: *You wear it, you wash it, and you wear it again! You won't need new clothes if you take care of ya old ones!*

Big Lenny had chosen to accompany Marshall and DeAngelo, his two youngest sons, here to Chicago, knowing they were going to retaliate for their big brother's murder and wanting to be there with them when they did it to make sure they got away with it.

Big Lenny reached into the pouch pocket in the bib of his overalls and brought out a pack of Newport 100's. Apparently Big Lenny hadn't quit smoking after all, bad heart or not. Still, it seemed to Marshall as if maybe the old man had cut down drastically, because that pack of Newports looked as if it had done hard traveling. It had escaped the short-lived fate of most packs, torn open after breakfast and tossed empty into the trash at three, a crushed ball. Big Lenny rummaged, brought out a cigarette almost as bent as the pack from which it had come. He stuck it in the corner of his mouth, replaced the pack in the bib, and brought out a chrome Zippo lighter which he rolled alight with one practice flick of his old man's thick calloused thumb. Marshall watched with the fascination of a child who watches a magician produce a rabbit from an empty top hat. How could a man smoke after being warned by his doctor that one more cigarette might mean an untimely death? And how could a man seem so calm the morning after his junior had been murdered?

They were in the living of Marshall's girlfriend's house, which could not have stood in a more convenient location. It was smack-dub in the middle of Drake Avenue, across the street and a couple of houses north from the building where Shawnna and Dawn Wilkins lived. It was also convenient that Marshall's girlfriend hated the Wilkins twins. They had jumped her at a strip club a few months back, and she wanted revenge. *Today.*

Her name was Chandra, and she was sitting beside Marshall on her couch. DeAngelo was standing next to the couch, peeking out through the blinds, holding an AK-47 assault rifle barrel-up on his shoulder, looking like that infamous photo of Malcolm X peering out at some unseen enemy.

"I know I ain't supposed to be smokin'," Big Lenny said, "and I ain't gon' tell you to lie or even ask you to. If your mama asks you 'was that old man smokin' in Chicago?' you go and tell her I was. I don't need nobody to lie for me." He didn't smile, but his shrewd, Mediterranean brown eyes made Marshall feel part of a conspiracy that seemed amiable and sinless. "But then, if ya mama asks *me* if you two came back here and did anything other than go with me to identify your brother's body, I'll look her right in the eye and say, 'No, ma'am. They drove me to that morgue and waited in the car while I went in and got a look at our boy, and that was *all* they done.' " The old man grinned, revealing his few remaining teeth. "Course, if she don't ask neither of us nothing, I guess we don't have to *volunteer* nothing…ya dig, son?"

"I ain't gon' say shit, Pops," Marshall said. He wasn't a good-looking young man and would probably never become the sort of man women exactly considered handsome, and with his nose swollen and twisted disproportionately between black-rimmed eyes, he thought he looked even less desirable.

"So, she hit you and Lenny with a set of brass knuckles, son?"

"Yep," Marshall lied, because he was too embarrassed by the truth.

"And you believe she had Lenny killed?"

"Yep. Her pops runs this whole neighborhood. She said she was gon' get bro killed a few hours before it happened."

"So, there's no question about this."

"None at all, Pops."

His father stood ruminating, his Newport burning with unnatural rapidity (the tobacco was dry, and although he puffed seldom, the greedy air blowing from Chandra's table-mounted fan smoked the cigarette ceaselessly), and Marshall thought the old man had said everything he had to say. He hoped not. He loved to hear Pops talk. The things Big Lenny said continually amazed him because they almost always made sense. Big Lenny was originally from right here in Chicago on the south side, an old school Gangster Disciple who had run the streets with some of the GD's founders back in the days of his youth. He was the reason his sons were Gangster Disciples.

The old man brooded down at his shoes for a moment. Marshall looked at him, slightly worried about the cigarette but very much liking the wild way the old man's gray hair blew around his head. At last Big Lenny looked up and shook his head, not somberly, but with brisk, almost humorous dismissiveness.

"I don't usually condone hurting women - 'No women, no kids,' that was always our motto - but if she did what you say she did, then she deserves what's coming to her. I'd rather take it out on the father, but she's the one who's ultimately responsible for your brother's murder, so we'll take her out."

Marshall nodded.

"What we'll do is…I'll go out to the car and pull it around back," Big Lenny said, and puffed his cigarette. "When you see her come out, you and DeAngelo run out the back door——"

"The *back* door?" Marshall asked.

"The back door," the old man confirmed. "You don't want them knowing you came out of here. You go out the back door, run around the side of here to the front yard, and open up on 'em." He raised an imaginary assault rifle. "Rat-tat-tat. Then run back around to the alley, jump in the car, and I get us back to the D. You got that?"

Marshall nodded again.

"Yep," DeAngelo said. He didn't look back. He kept his eyes on the building across the way, not even nodding, so focused was he. Pops nodded for both of them and knocked a roll of ash off his cigarette.

"No need in letting loose a whole shitstorm of bullets," the old man said, putting on his leather bomber jacket. "Just get the job done and get to the car. We need to be on the move as soon as we can move. I ain't lookin' to go back to the joint. I ain't got another bid in me." He zipped up the jacket with his right eye shut to keep the cigarette smoke out of it.

Marshall stood up, leaving his own Ak-47 on the couch. He walked over and gave the old man a hug. "I'm doing this for Lenny Jr.," he said. "He ain't about to be the only one getting buried."

"Sho' in the hell ain't," Big Lenny said, pulling free from Marshall's embrace and strolling to the door. He patted DeAngelo twice on the shoulder and then out the door he went.

For a long moment, Marshall stood in the exact same spot where his father had stood, gazing at DeAngelo, who seemed to have been frozen in place at the window. Lenny Jr. was dead. He was dead, and there would be no bringing him back. It was a hard pill to swallow. Marshall had counted on big bro for just about everything.

"You all right?" Chandra asked.

Marshall nodded. "I'm ready to get this shit over with and get back to Detroit with my folks."

"Just make sure you get that bitch Shawnna. I hope you can hit her *and* Dawn, but Shawnna's the real problem. She's the ringleader. I hope y'all shoot that bitch all in the face."

A small grin appeared on Marshall's battered face. He and Chandra had the same hopes. He was just about to tell her this when DeAngelo spun away from the window, picked up Marshall's assault rifle, and tossed it to him.

"Let's go," DeAngelo said, and the two brothers bolted to the back door, snatching the hoods of their sweaters up over their heads.

Neither brother spoke as they began to descend the snow-coated wooden stairs on the back porch. Marshall went left, DeAngelo right. Marshall could hear and feel the snow crushing under his feet. The wind guard, blowing his hood around his bruised face, then dropped away completely. When it did, he heard the distinct growl of Big Lenny's well-kept Chevy Camaro moving carefully into the alleyway. That familiar sound gave him the dose of adrenaline he needed to soldier on through the heavy snow, which rose to the top of his calves alongside Chandra's house, where no snowplow or shovel come to clear the way. He was about halfway to the front of the redbrick house when the snow became his enemy. He had just taken a step with his right foot and was lifting his left leg out of the deep white when it happened. His left foot didn't fully clear the icy hole, and he fell forwards. As he did, his fingers reflexively tightened around the assault rifle, and he accidentally pulled the trigger.

The gunshot was loud, like a crack of thunder.

"Shit," Marshall said, struggling to get back to his feet.

Before he could get his feet under him, somebody - or maybe a few somebodies, he couldn't say for sure - let loose a whole shitstorm of bullets.

Chapter 21

It had been decided: Shawnna and Reese would transport the duffle bags full of cash to Lake Forest, since Reese's assistant was already going there to spend Christmas with Bubbles, and Dawn was going to Jamaica with her new love interest.

Shawnna was standing on the front porch with Dawn and Shay, listening as Shay revealed that she was also a twin and that her twin had been murdered a couple of years ago, when a sudden clap of gunfire murdered their conversation.

Wayno had been helping Chubb and Reese load the three duffels into the Bentayga's rear storage compartment. Upon hearing the gunshot, all three of them reached into their coats and brought out their pistols. Chubb's looked like a replica of RoboCop's gun, and Reese's was the only one with an extended magazine, which he'd refilled to its full capacity shortly after Shawnna's early morning meltdown.

"Y'all go in the house," Reese shouted as he and the other two began to scan the street.

But the door was locked, and Shawnna didn't think it wise to turn her back to the street when she'd just heard what a high-caliber gun was clearly go off. Still, she fished in her Gucci bag for the keys, looking from one end of Drake Avenue to the other. A group of teenage boys - TVL's her father had ordered to secure the stretch of Drake between 16th and 18th streets (there was no 17th - came running down the sidewalk from the corner of 18th.

Dawn had very sharp eyes and it wasn't really surprising that she was the first to discover the hooded gunman creeping out from beside a house across the street.

"Next to Chandra's house!" Dawn shrieked, pointing.

What Shawnna saw beyond the tip of her twin sister's pointing finger sucked all the air from her lungs.

The gunman was raising an AK-47, and it didn't take Shawnna but half a second to see that the dark-faced man was taking aim at the porch she was standing on, while Reese and the gang were taking aim at him.

Shawnna saw the AK-47 flash, and just as she heard the gigantic boom and felt a searing heat streak past her left ear, Dawn tackled her to the ground. She landed on her ass. Hard. But her eyes remained on the gunman, even as the bricks around the door behind her began to explode and rain down on her head, a cloudy mixture of brick and mortar. She saw the mists of blood spray out of him as he was shot down, and she found it strange how he stayed focused on her until a bullet hit his head and took him down for good.

Then there was more gunfire. One by one, the windows in Wayno's long red Chevy Suburban began to shatter. The firepower rocked the SUV on its wheels.

I'm about to die on Christmas, Shawnna thought.

Dawn tried to scream, but shock rubbed her voice and she was able to produce only a low, choked whuffling - the sound of a woman moaning in her sleep. She drew in breath to try it again, but before she could get started, Shawnna's hand seized her left arm just below the elbow in a strong pincer grip and squeezed.

"No-no-no-no-no," an urgent voice said. It took a second for Shawnna to realize that it was her own voice. It was pitched only half a step above a whisper, and it spoke directly into Dawn's left ear. "Don't let them hear you! We're the targets! We're the fucking targets!"

Chapter 22

Blake played with the kids until he was all played out. He strapped his one-year-old into a miniature Ferrari and used a remote control to take little Juan on a journey through the Calabasas mansion's vast expense of marble-floored rooms. Juan's two big brothers drove alongside him in their own mini Ferraris. It was Juan's first mini car, but Blake King Jr. and King Neal Costilla had dozens of them.

By noontime the kids were ready for a nap - the boys were, at least. Blake's daughter was nine and in her mind, that meant nineteen. Savaria hadn't done much since opening her presents. She had flown her new drone outside for about an hour, accompanied by Alexus, but since then, she'd been in her bedroom, trying on her new clothes and modeling them for Alexus and Rita. Blake wasn't at all surprised by the blatant segregation; Vari considered boys to be the most disgusting creatures on the planet, and Beyoncé had long ago convinced her that all ladies needed to stick together and get in formation. She loved her little brothers, but she loved them from a distance. She liked to wear a lot of white, like Alexus, and her little brothers had nasty little fingers that were often sticky with sugar and chocolates.

Blake put the boys to bed and then went outside and sat in his car - a triple black Bugatti Veyron convertible - to smoke a blunt of Kush and relax his mind. He was just lighting up when Alexus came sauntering out of the mansion's ten-foot double-doors, smiling a perfect smile that seemed to be veiling a different look.

"Gonna smoke up the Christmas tree without me?" Alexus asked as she poured herself into the passenger's seat beside him, an angel in a white dress.

Blake took a hard pull on the blunt. "No more kids for me," he said, in the stuffy voice of a man whose lungs are inflated with weed smoke. "Four is more than enough for the both of us."

"We can always adopt."

"Adopt these nuts."

She flipped him two middle fingers, grinning. "Asshole," she said, and rolled her sexy green eyes way up in their sockets. A second later, those emerald irises were back on him. She leaned toward him and pressed her lips against his cheek. "I'm sorry about flipping out on you over that stupid picture you took with Bubbles the other day. I really am. I don't know what I was thinking. I'm going to see Dr. Farr tomorrow. She's always a good voice of reason."

Blake only nodded and passed her the blunt. He had the top down and was slouched back in his seat, his eyes far off, studying a cloud that looked like a pitbull leaping at a short stick moving swiftly across the blue sky.

"Do you forgive me?" Alexus asked.

"I wouldn't be here if I didn't," Blake said. "Shit, I know how crazy yo' nutty ass is. I knew Papi, remember? And your crazy-ass aunt Jenny. Crazy runs in your family."

"Hey, my father wasn't crazy."

"Sure, he wasn't."

"You can't blame me for getting mad about seeing you with your arm around a bitch's shoulder when she's the same bitch you fucked every time we separated. I don't think that makes me crazy. What would you do if I took a picture with some guy I used to fuck? Huh? What if I took a picture with my arm around T-Walk?"

Blake turned his head so fast his vertebrae almost snapped. He stared coldly at Alexus, gritting his teeth together, nostrils flaring like a police K-9 in a trap house. She crossed her arms defiantly.

"See what I mean?" Alexus said.

"Don't get fucked up," Blake said tightly.

"Oh, so it would be wrong if I did it, but it's fine when you do it?"

"You can't compare that shit. Me and that nigga T-Walk went to war. I whacked a gang of his niggas, and he whacked a gang of mine. I shot him, and he shot me. That's way different. If you hug that nigga you might as well move in with him or move him in with you."

Alexus sucked her teeth. She sat back, gave his blunt back to him, and rolled her eyes again. He kept staring at her, puffing his Kush and staring at her perfect face and wondering if she'd lost her mother fucking mind on this warm, beautiful Christmas in Calabasas.

"It happened when I bonded out of jail the other night," she muttered with her eyes cast straight forward. "When I took Bubbles and her two friends to dinner at my restaurant. He followed the paparazzi to the restaurant, came in, asked me for a hug, and then left. Somebody took a picture without my knowledge. The Shade Room posted the pic late last night. It went viral immediately, which isn't really surprising. Everybody wants to see us fall apart now that T-Walk is back. That's why I didn't want you on your phone. I didn't want you to see the picture."

Blake threw back his head and chuckled at the cloud that looked like a pitbull. That cloud, the stick part now stretched as long as a flagpole, had gotten itself halfway from one horizon to the other.

"Where's my phone?" Blake said, forcing himself to remain calm.

She reached her hand into the top of her dress and pulled his iPhone out from under her left breast. He snatched it out of her hand, found the photo on Instagram, and looked at it. He nodded, left Instagram, and sent Savaria a text message telling her to come outside.

"I'm sorry, Blake. All it was was a hug, I swear on Papi's grave that's all it was, but I'm sorry for letting it happen." Alexus's eyes were gleaming with tears.

"Will you get out so my daughter can get in?"

"Blake, please..." Alexus began to cry. Not just tears, but really boohooing. She reached for him, and he shoved her back. "Don't do this to me, Blake. Please. We're married."

"I ain't tryna hear that shit. Go marry T-Walk. You wanna hug him so bad, go on and marry him." The anger was pulsing through Blake in slow, throbbing waves.

Savaria came out of the enormous mansion wearing an expensive white jumpsuit and a mile-wide smile that slowly shrunk as she approached the Bugatti. Alexus gazed at Blake through her tears for a moment, reluctant to exit the car, but finally she did.

"What's wrong, Ma?" Vari asked, but Alexus was already walking off, headed back into the mansion, so Vari turned to Blake. "Daddy, what's wrong with her?"

"She ain't loyal." Blake started the powerful engine and smashed his blunt out in the ashtray, revolving it from left to right until it was no longer smoking. "She ain't never been loyal. Forget about her. It's just me and you again."

"I'm with you right or wrong, Daddy," Vari said, engaging her seatbelt.

Blake raced out of the driveway. If Alexus wanted to play these ex-games, he would play them right along with her. He thumbed through the list of saved contacts in his iPhone and tried to decide on who he wanted to call first.

Tasia "Baddie Barbie" Olsen, an exotic dancer in Atlanta, was the first to come to mind. Then he considered Lakita "Bubbles" Thomas.

I'll call 'em both, he thought.

To Be Continued...
The Brick Man 5
Coming Soon

Lock Down Publications and Ca$h Presents assisted publishing packages.

BASIC PACKAGE $499
Editing
Cover Design
Formatting

UPGRADED PACKAGE $800
Typing
Editing
Cover Design
Formatting

ADVANCE PACKAGE $1,200
Typing
Editing
Cover Design
Formatting
Copyright registration
Proofreading
Upload book to Amazon

LDP SUPREME PACKAGE $1,500
Typing
Editing
Cover Design
Formatting
Copyright registration

Proofreading
Set up Amazon account
Upload book to Amazon
Advertise on LDP Amazon and Facebook page

***Other services available upon request. Additional
charges may apply
Lock Down Publications
P.O. Box 944
Stockbridge, GA 30281-9998
Phone # 470 303-9761

Submission Guideline

Submit the first three chapters of your completed manuscript to ldpsubmissions@gmail.com, subject line: Your book's title. The manuscript must be in a .doc file and sent as an attachment. Document should be in Times New Roman, double spaced and in size 12 font. Also, provide your synopsis and full contact information. If sending multiple submissions, they must each be in a separate email.

Have a story but no way to send it electronically? You can still submit to LDP/Ca$h Presents. Send in the first three chapters, written or typed, of your completed manuscript to:

LDP: Submissions Dept
Po Box 944
Stockbridge, Ga 30281

DO NOT send original manuscript. Must be a duplicate.

Provide your synopsis and a cover letter containing your full contact information.

Thanks for considering LDP and Ca$h Presents.

NEW RELEASES

FOR THE LOVE OF BLOOD by JAMEL
MITCHELL
CONCRETE KILLA 3 by KINGPEN
RAN OFF ON DA PLUG by PAPER BOI RARI
THE BRICK MAN 4 by KING RIO

3X KRAZY III

STRAIGHT BEAST MODE II

De'Kari

KINGPIN KILLAZ IV

STREET KINGS III

PAID IN BLOOD III

CARTEL KILLAZ IV

DOPE GODS III

Hood Rich

SINS OF A HUSTLA II

ASAD

RICH $AVAGE II

By Martell Troublesome Bolden

YAYO V

Bred In The Game 2

S. Allen

CREAM III

THE STREETS WILL TALK II

By Yolanda Moore

SON OF A DOPE FIEND III

HEAVEN GOT A GHETTO II

By Renta

LOYALTY AIN'T PROMISED III

By Keith Williams

I'M NOTHING WITHOUT HIS LOVE II

SINS OF A THUG II

TO THE THUG I LOVED BEFORE II

IN A HUSTLER I TRUST II

By Monet Dragun

QUIET MONEY IV

EXTENDED CLIP III

THUG LIFE IV

By **Trai'Quan**

THE STREETS MADE ME IV

By **Larry D. Wright**

IF YOU CROSS ME ONCE II

By **Anthony Fields**

THE STREETS WILL NEVER CLOSE IV

By K'ajji

HARD AND RUTHLESS III

KILLA KOUNTY III

By Khufu

MONEY GAME III

By Smoove Dolla

JACK BOYS VS DOPE BOYS II

A GANGSTA'S QUR'AN V

COKE GIRLZ II

By Romell Tukes

MURDA WAS THE CASE II

Elijah R. Freeman

THE STREETS NEVER LET GO II

By Robert Baptiste

AN UNFORESEEN LOVE III

By **Meesha**

KING OF THE TRENCHES III

by **GHOST & TRANAY ADAMS**

MONEY MAFIA II

LOYAL TO THE SOIL III

By **Jibril Williams**

QUEEN OF THE ZOO II

By **Black Migo**

VICIOUS LOYALTY III

By Kingpen

A GANGSTA'S PAIN III

By J-Blunt

CONFESSIONS OF A JACKBOY III

By Nicholas Lock

GRIMEY WAYS II

By Ray Vinci

KING KILLA II

By Vincent "Vitto" Holloway

BETRAYAL OF A THUG II

By Fre$h

THE MURDER QUEENS II

By Michael Gallon

THE BIRTH OF A GANGSTER II

By Delmont Player

TREAL LOVE II

By Le'Monica Jackson

FOR THE LOVE OF BLOOD II

By Jamel Mitchell

King Rio

RAN OFF ON DA PLUG II

By Paper Boi Rari

Available Now

RESTRAINING ORDER **I & II**

By **CA$H & Coffee**

LOVE KNOWS NO BOUNDARIES **I II & III**

By **Coffee**

RAISED AS A GOON I, II, III & IV

BRED BY THE SLUMS I, II, III

BLAST FOR ME I & II

ROTTEN TO THE CORE I II III

A BRONX TALE I, II, III

DUFFLE BAG CARTEL I II III IV V VI

HEARTLESS GOON I II III IV V

A SAVAGE DOPEBOY I II

DRUG LORDS I II III

CUTTHROAT MAFIA I II

KING OF THE TRENCHES

By **Ghost**

LAY IT DOWN **I & II**

LAST OF A DYING BREED I II

BLOOD STAINS OF A SHOTTA I & II III

By **Jamaica**

LOYAL TO THE GAME I II III

LIFE OF SIN I, II III

By **TJ & Jelissa**

BLOODY COMMAS I & II

SKI MASK CARTEL I II & III

KING OF NEW YORK I II,III IV V

RISE TO POWER I II III

COKE KINGS I II III IV V

BORN HEARTLESS I II III IV

KING OF THE TRAP I II

By **T.J. Edwards**

IF LOVING HIM IS WRONG…I & II

LOVE ME EVEN WHEN IT HURTS I II III

By **Jelissa**

WHEN THE STREETS CLAP BACK I & II III

THE HEART OF A SAVAGE I II III

MONEY MAFIA

LOYAL TO THE SOIL I II

By **Jibril Williams**

A DISTINGUISHED THUG STOLE MY HEART I II & III

LOVE SHOULDN'T HURT I II III IV

RENEGADE BOYS I II III IV

PAID IN KARMA I II III

SAVAGE STORMS I II III

AN UNFORESEEN LOVE I II

By **Meesha**

A GANGSTER'S CODE I &, II III

A GANGSTER'S SYN I II III

THE SAVAGE LIFE I II III

CHAINED TO THE STREETS I II III

BLOOD ON THE MONEY I II III

A GANGSTA'S PAIN I II

By J-Blunt

PUSH IT TO THE LIMIT

By **Bre' Hayes**

BLOOD OF A BOSS **I, II, III, IV, V**

SHADOWS OF THE GAME

TRAP BASTARD

By **Askari**

THE STREETS BLEED MURDER **I, II & III**

THE HEART OF A GANGSTA I II& III

By **Jerry Jackson**

CUM FOR ME I II III IV V VI VII VIII

An **LDP Erotica Collaboration**

BRIDE OF A HUSTLA **I II & II**

THE FETTI GIRLS **I, II& III**

CORRUPTED BY A GANGSTA I, II III, IV

BLINDED BY HIS LOVE

THE PRICE YOU PAY FOR LOVE I, II ,III

DOPE GIRL MAGIC I II III

The Brick Man 4

By **Destiny Skai**

WHEN A GOOD GIRL GOES BAD

By **Adrienne**

THE COST OF LOYALTY I II III

By Kweli

A GANGSTER'S REVENGE **I II III & IV**

THE BOSS MAN'S DAUGHTERS I II III IV V

A SAVAGE LOVE **I & II**

BAE BELONGS TO ME I II

A HUSTLER'S DECEIT I, II, III

WHAT BAD BITCHES DO I, II, III

SOUL OF A MONSTER I II III

KILL ZONE

A DOPE BOY'S QUEEN I II III

By **Aryanna**

A KINGPIN'S AMBITON

A KINGPIN'S AMBITION **II**

I MURDER FOR THE DOUGH

By **Ambitious**

TRUE SAVAGE I II III IV V VI VII

DOPE BOY MAGIC I, II, III

MIDNIGHT CARTEL I II III

CITY OF KINGZ I II

NIGHTMARE ON SILENT AVE

THE PLUG OF LIL MEXICO II

By **Chris Green**

A DOPEBOY'S PRAYER

By **Eddie "Wolf" Lee**

THE KING CARTEL **I, II & III**

By **Frank Gresham**

THESE NIGGAS AIN'T LOYAL **I, II & III**

By **Nikki Tee**

GANGSTA SHYT **I II &III**

By **CATO**

THE ULTIMATE BETRAYAL

By **Phoenix**

BOSS'N UP **I , II & III**

By **Royal Nicole**

I LOVE YOU TO DEATH

By **Destiny J**

I RIDE FOR MY HITTA

I STILL RIDE FOR MY HITTA

By **Misty Holt**

LOVE & CHASIN' PAPER

By **Qay Crockett**

TO DIE IN VAIN

SINS OF A HUSTLA

By **ASAD**

BROOKLYN HUSTLAZ

By **Boogsy Morina**

BROOKLYN ON LOCK I & II

By **Sonovia**

GANGSTA CITY

By **Teddy Duke**

A DRUG KING AND HIS DIAMOND I & II III

A DOPEMAN'S RICHES

HER MAN, MINE'S TOO I, II

CASH MONEY HO'S

THE WIFEY I USED TO BE I II

By **Nicole Goosby**

TRAPHOUSE KING **I II & III**

KINGPIN KILLAZ I II III

STREET KINGS I II

PAID IN BLOOD **I II**

CARTEL KILLAZ I II III

DOPE GODS I II

By **Hood Rich**

LIPSTICK KILLAH **I, II, III**

CRIME OF PASSION I II & III

FRIEND OR FOE I II III

By **Mimi**

STEADY MOBBN' **I, II, III**

THE STREETS STAINED MY SOUL I II III

By **Marcellus Allen**

WHO SHOT YA **I, II, III**

SON OF A DOPE FIEND I II

HEAVEN GOT A GHETTO

Renta

GORILLAZ IN THE BAY **I II III IV**

TEARS OF A GANGSTA I II

3X KRAZY I II

STRAIGHT BEAST MODE

DE'KARI

TRIGGADALE I II III

MURDAROBER WAS THE CASE

Elijah R. Freeman

GOD BLESS THE TRAPPERS I, II, III

THESE SCANDALOUS STREETS I, II, III

FEAR MY GANGSTA I, II, III IV, V

THESE STREETS DON'T LOVE NOBODY I, II

BURY ME A G I, II, III, IV, V

A GANGSTA'S EMPIRE I, II, III, IV

THE DOPEMAN'S BODYGAURD I II

THE REALEST KILLAZ I II III

THE LAST OF THE OGS I II III

Tranay Adams

THE STREETS ARE CALLING

Duquie Wilson

MARRIED TO A BOSS I II III

By Destiny Skai & Chris Green

KINGZ OF THE GAME I II III IV V VI

Playa Ray

SLAUGHTER GANG I II III

RUTHLESS HEART I II III

By Willie Slaughter

FUK SHYT

By Blakk Diamond

DON'T F#CK WITH MY HEART I II

By Linnea

ADDICTED TO THE DRAMA I II III

IN THE ARM OF HIS BOSS II

By Jamila

YAYO I II III IV

A SHOOTER'S AMBITION I II

BRED IN THE GAME

By S. Allen

TRAP GOD I II III

RICH $AVAGE

MONEY IN THE GRAVE I II III

By Martell Troublesome Bolden

FOREVER GANGSTA

GLOCKS ON SATIN SHEETS I II

By Adrian Dulan

TOE TAGZ I II III IV

LEVELS TO THIS SHYT I II

By Ah'Million

KINGPIN DREAMS I II III

RAN OFF ON DA PLUG

By Paper Boi Rari

CONFESSIONS OF A GANGSTA I II III IV

CONFESSIONS OF A JACKBOY I II

By Nicholas Lock

I'M NOTHING WITHOUT HIS LOVE

SINS OF A THUG

TO THE THUG I LOVED BEFORE

A GANGSTA SAVED XMAS

IN A HUSTLER I TRUST

By Monet Dragun

CAUGHT UP IN THE LIFE I II III

THE STREETS NEVER LET GO

By Robert Baptiste

NEW TO THE GAME I II III

MONEY, MURDER & MEMORIES I II III

By **Malik D. Rice**

LIFE OF A SAVAGE I II III

A GANGSTA'S QUR'AN I II III IV

MURDA SEASON I II III

GANGLAND CARTEL I II III

CHI'RAQ GANGSTAS I II III

KILLERS ON ELM STREET I II III

JACK BOYZ N DA BRONX I II III

A DOPEBOY'S DREAM I II III

JACK BOYS VS DOPE BOYS

COKE GIRLZ

By Romell Tukes

LOYALTY AIN'T PROMISED I II

By Keith Williams

QUIET MONEY I II III

THUG LIFE I II III

EXTENDED CLIP I II

By **Trai'Quan**

THE STREETS MADE ME I II III

By **Larry D. Wright**

THE ULTIMATE SACRIFICE I, II, III, IV, V, VI

KHADIFI

IF YOU CROSS ME ONCE

ANGEL I II

IN THE BLINK OF AN EYE

By **Anthony Fields**

THE LIFE OF A HOOD STAR

By **Ca$h & Rashia Wilson**

THE STREETS WILL NEVER CLOSE I II III

By **K'ajji**

CREAM I II

THE STREETS WILL TALK

By **Yolanda Moore**

NIGHTMARES OF A HUSTLA I II III

By **King Dream**

CONCRETE KILLA I II III

VICIOUS LOYALTY I II

By **Kingpen**

HARD AND RUTHLESS I II

MOB TOWN 251

THE BILLIONAIRE BENTLEYS I II III

By **Von Diesel**

GHOST MOB

Stilloan Robinson

MOB TIES I II III IV V VI

King Rio

By SayNoMore

BODYMORE MURDERLAND I II III

THE BIRTH OF A GANGSTER

By Delmont Player

FOR THE LOVE OF A BOSS

By C. D. Blue

MOBBED UP I II III IV

THE BRICK MAN I II III IV

THE COCAINE PRINCESS I II III IV V

By King Rio

KILLA KOUNTY I II III

By Khufu

MONEY GAME I II

By Smoove Dolla

A GANGSTA'S KARMA I II

By FLAME

KING OF THE TRENCHES I II

by **GHOST & TRANAY ADAMS**

QUEEN OF THE ZOO

By **Black Migo**

GRIMEY WAYS

By Ray Vinci

XMAS WITH AN ATL SHOOTER

By Ca$h & Destiny Skai

KING KILLA

By Vincent "Vitto" Holloway

BETRAYAL OF A THUG

By Fre$h

THE MURDER QUEENS

By Michael Gallon

TREAL LOVE

By Le'Monica Jackson

FOR THE LOVE OF BLOOD

By Jamel Mitchell

<u>BOOKS BY LDP'S CEO, CA$H</u>

TRUST IN NO MAN

TRUST IN NO MAN 2

TRUST IN NO MAN 3

BONDED BY BLOOD

SHORTY GOT A THUG

THUGS CRY

THUGS CRY 2

THUGS CRY 3

TRUST NO BITCH

TRUST NO BITCH 2

TRUST NO BITCH 3

TIL MY CASKET DROPS

RESTRAINING ORDER

RESTRAINING ORDER 2

IN LOVE WITH A CONVICT

LIFE OF A HOOD STAR

XMAS WITH AN ATL SHOOTER

The Brick Man 4